# PE
# JA
# RUSSELL

# The Drawing Board

"Crimes of passion rarely make sense, that's why they're called crimes of passion.
If they made sense, then they'd be called crimes of reason."

Also By Peter James Russell

**My Choice Of Words**

**Clearing My Throat. Selected Poems**

For Jean and Tom.

"We're living in a unique time in which ordinary citizens around the world are collaborating to understand and expose the corrupt system that rules us. The system thrives on deception, and the overwhelming task of The Great Awakening is to penetrate its lies and reveal the truth."

Qanon

# 1. Fiona

"Do you take this man to be your wedded husband?"
The bride turned her head, not towards her expectant groom, but instead to look the other way, at her mother. As if for some final confirmation that she did, or that she should.
"To cherish in love and in friendship, in strength and in weakness."
Fiona's mother had never been married, although her father had. His current wife was his fourth.
"In success and in disappointment, to love him for as long as the two of you shall live?"
He was not in church today. He had declined the invitation, excusing himself with the fact that it was a long journey to make from Bangalore at such short notice. But he had written a long and warm letter to his daughter. And he had sent her a generous sum of money to pay for her dress, and for the reception. Neither of which she did.
The groom's father was absent too, having died when his son was not yet three years old. Geert had hardly any memory of him. He had been raised by his mother, her sisters, and their parents, all of whom were very much present and correct today.
"And do you take this woman to be your wedded wife? To cherish in love and in friendship, in strength and in weakness?"
Fiona and her mother answered for him, silently, separately, and to themselves, not wishing to be rude, or to give the game away.
The joke was from a country song that both were fond of. It was called 'She's No Lady She's My Wife' and the singer, an urbane, if rather odd looking, Texan by the name of Lyle Lovett, had once, briefly, been married to Julia Roberts.
Last night at Fiona's bachelorette party, or her hen party, to use the English idiom that Fiona, after all of her three years in London, now favoured, they watched the clip of it together again for the umpteenth time. And they, and Fiona's bridesmaids, one, a colleague from the gallery where she worked, and where she first met Geert, the other two, her housemates, all new to country music and to its capacity for humour, all laughed heartily.
By then, Geert's Mother, her sisters, and the mysterious redhead who

1

had been introduced only as a family friend, but who was clearly an ex of Geert's who still held a torch for him, had all long since made their excuses and left the party.

In the circumstances, it was probably just as well. For although many a true word is spoken in jest, the bride's boast that she was marrying Geert because she could, would most likely not have gone down as well with them as it had with her own entourage.

"It's like rock stars and models" she explained. "Or country singers and actresses" her mother said, raising another glass of champagne to her daughter.

"Or art students and investment bankers" one of her housemates added, making the joke unnecessarily literal, and so a little cruel, Fiona thought. Fiona's mother was having the time of her long and varied life. She had taken a month's vacation from work and her ticket had been a gift from her employers.

It was her first trip to Europe. She had arrived ten days ago and had stood in the crowd outside Westminster Abbey at William and Kate's Wedding only last Saturday.

She had, in fact, spent the three months since the engagement telling friends and colleagues that she was off to London for 'the wedding'. Mother, like daughter, seeing nothing wrong in letting people take more from what was said than what was meant.

She had been raised on a smallholding in West Texas in a family of originally German Lutheran descent. By the age of eighteen, having already had more than enough of her parents strict religious observance, and although still a child under state law, she ran away to San Francisco.

It was The Summer of Love, and as thousands like her from all over the US and beyond, she joined a commune and became a flower child. She waited table and worked in record stores before taking a job first as a flight attendant, and then in HR for an airline company in Seattle.

By the time Fiona was born, her relationship with Fiona's father, an Indian aerospace engineer, had ended. He returned to India, to his arranged marriage soon after.

Fiona grew up in a rented two bed bungalow in Beacon Hill on the South edge of the city. A family neighbourhood of woods and parks and yoga studios and organic cafes, from where, in summer, or when the winter fog cleared, you could see Mount Rainier.

The only child of a single mother, she felt at home among its American Asian community, without ever particularly feeling that she belonged to it. Riding her bike to the International School, where she studied well enough without excelling or disappointing. And hanging with her mom and her friends on weekends.

Her father supported her education and from her early pre-teens would also pay for her to visit him in India at least once a year. Or else he would come to Seattle, where he still had friends, and occasionally still did business.

Her childhood was happy enough for her to have never really given it much thought. She certainly never felt any animosity between her separated parents or any conflict between their separate lives.

In fact, as she grew up, she felt increasingly fortunate to have both. And when the time came for her to graduate High School it was no great surprise that, rather than continue to pursue a college education, she would take some time out to travel.

And so, via a year in India, a couple of years en route to Europe and three years in Amsterdam, here she was in London. Studying History of Art at Goldsmiths College, working at a gallery in Peckham, and sharing a house with the two young women who now stood beside her at the altar of St. James.

The bride and groom had met, not quite a year ago, at a verntisage for the first solo show by a young man who was a Goldsmiths graduate, and a friend of Fiona's.

The owner of the gallery's wife was Dutch and there was some family connection with Geert. He had no great interest in art, but he was single, and had therefore made the lengthy trip south of the river from Highgate in the hope of maybe meeting someone.

Perhaps it was in the stars, perhaps it was the champagne. Perhaps it was a bit of both, and a bit more of other things besides, but here he was now standing at the altar of a church in Peckham with the very someone that he had hoped to meet that night.

The woman who he had seen through the window before he even set foot in the gallery that night, the woman whom he had assumed must be the artist's girlfriend.

The woman who had taken him by surprise when she had taken him by the arm and kissed his cheek and then introduced herself in Dutch.

The woman who he had spent the winter months with walking together in Waterlow Park or across Hampstead Heath for Sunday lunch at The Holly Bush.

The woman who had, entirely out of the blue, asked him to be her husband.

The woman to whom he now said I do, and who said I do to him.

3

The woman about whom his mother, and his aunts, and his grandparents, all still had many questions that remained to them unanswered by those two words.

The woman who knew though, that, for now at least, they were a sufficient answer to the question do you? If not to the question why do you?

The answer to that was more complicated than 'because I can'. It was not that she was as calculating as Geert's family feared, or that she was as impulsive as she often seemed.

And surely, it was not possible to be both at the same time.

Her proposal of marriage had not come out of the blue. She had known that Geert would be her lover from the moment she first saw him.

He had never hidden his wish to be a father or have a son. And she knew that he would make a good one. That much was simply intuition.

And intuition is not the same thing as impulse, nor is it a quality exclusive to women.

Geert had accepted her proposal on not much more than his intuition. Which had, professionally at least, always served him well enough so far.

There was also the not unimportant fact that they were in love with each other. That each believed, as sincerely as only young people can, that they had found each others missing half, by chance, one evening in a gallery in Peckham.

And besides, since love is something that is best left to grow unquestioned, perhaps the answer to the question why was really not so complicated after all.

Perhaps, in fact, it was simply another question, why not?

## 2. Frank

She did not make love, she had told him soon after they met, she fucked. She was Dutch. As careful with her emotions as she was with her money, and equally keen to talk loudly about both. But she fucked enthusiastically, if not as often as he would have wished. She had, on one occasion, fucked him at gunpoint. Which was not something that was easily forgotten. But Dutch tomato soup, as Belgians say, more often than not turns out to be hot water in a red bowl.

Frank let the thought pass. He finished his Lait Russe, placed his tray on the rack in the corner, bid a Bonne Journee to the waitress, and left the cafeteria.

But that was the problem, there were no good days, there were no bad days either, just days, hundreds and hundreds of them, each the same as the one before and the one after.

Force of habit would now dictate that Frank would take a cigarette on the terrace, but, without really looking, today he sensed the lurking presence of Renaud, a man whom he utterly detested.

Their workplace aside, mutual antipathy, and smoking, seemed to be the only two things that the two men had in common. More than once, Frank had seen himself approach the diminutive Frenchman and, on the pretext of asking for a light, lift him by the lapels and hurl him onto the train tracks below.

In his dreams, but now he thought of it, had he maybe mentioned it to someone?

The need for nicotine, powerful as it was, could not overpower his aversion to a moment longer of exposure to Renaud's psychopathic gaze than was professionally necessary.

He would instead return to his office on the sixth floor for long enough to know that he had been seen there, and then he would return to the terrace to smoke in peace.

The elevator door closed behind him. He was alone. He checked his eyes in the mirror. You could tell the undead by their eyes, and whenever he could, Frank liked to take the opportunity to confirm that he had not yet joined them.

Frank McDonald was an only child. His mother had spent much of his childhood and adolescence in a succession of psychiatric institutions.

Before taking her own life during the last long summer vacation that Frank spent at home before going to university. He was sixteen.

If it were ever mentioned, Frank liked to say that he had been brought up by his father, but the truth was that, in reality, Frank had been brought up by himself.

Every Saturday morning since the first that he could remember, his father left the house at dawn to be ready on the first tee at first light for the day's first eighteen holes of golf.

The adolescent Frank passed most of his weekends in bed, either reading, or listening to the radio, but never both at the same time. From that day to this, whatever it was that occupied his mind occupied it completely.

Then it was music. And football, which his father considered to be not only vulgar, but dangerous. Too dangerous certainly for a sensitive child like Frank to ever be allowed to attend a game; music, and football, and history.

When not reading or listening to the radio, he slept, and he dreamed. Looking back on his childhood, which he did regularly and frequently, it was as if those days had been spent in suspended animation.

Or else something akin to a form of hibernation, a state of mind, or the absence of a state of mind, that had stayed with him in adulthood.

Something that was, coincidentally or not, entirely suited to the only job that Frank had ever had, or was ever likely to have, that of a Brussels functionary. A job for life, if not longer, to which admittance is gained by competitive examination.

That Frank had always been good at exams was down to his good fortune in having been taught History by Mr Galbraith, Peter Galbraith to his colleagues at Irvine Royal Academy.

Mental Pete to those he took his place with at Rugby Park on a Saturday afternoon and drank with on the buses to stand on the terraces at Aberdeen or Dundee or Inverness Caledonian Thistle or Queen of The South, come rain, hail, or occasional shine.

Frank and Mr Galbraith shared a devotion to Kilmarnock FC, and to history, and to the history of football, and to the history of Scottish football in particular. It was the Scots, as Mr Galbraith had frequently reminded him and as Frank now frequently reminded others, who had invented the game, and had exported it, first to England, and then to Brazil.

It was the Scots who invented the dugout, and the season ticket, and who perfected the modern game of running and passing. It was a Scottish architect, Archibald Leitch, who not only built Ibrox, but also Anfield,

6

Highbury, Old Trafford and Stamford Bridge and a dozen or more others. It was a Scottish player, Andrew Watson, the son of a plantation owner in British Guyana, who was the first person of colour ever to play the professional game in Britain, captaining Scotland to famous victories over England and Wales.

And it was a fact that no country on earth could boast more professional football clubs per head of population than Scotland, nor more people regularly attending their games.

As well as a detailed knowledge of football, and the importance of their countrymen in its history, Mr Galbraith had impressed upon the teenage Frank the importance of exams. And the fact that excelling in them has little to do with what you know, and much more to do with what you can manage to persuade the examiner to believe you know.

From Irvine Royal Academy, through his Bachelor's at Glasgow University, his first Masters at Oxford, his second at Leuven, his Doctorate at Utrecht, and finally, his EU Concourse, exams had never been something that had ever stood in Frank's way.

As time passed, and his father was no longer in a position to prohibit him from joining Mental Pete on the terraces, master and pupil had grown to become friends. Sharing the ups, and the mostly downs, of Kilmarnock FC and the Scottish National Team together whenever they could

Together they had revelled in the heady euphoria of Killie's third-place finish in The Scottish Premiership in the second year of Steve Clarke's managerial tenure.

Clarke, from up the road in Saltcoats, had won trophies at Stamford Bridge as a player, and then risen through the coaching ranks to become Jose Mourinho's assistant.

Although only three years his senior, Clarke's unsmiling, Ayrshire manner reminded Frank of his father. But his quiet determination, and his talent for fashioning silk purses from sow's ears, had earned Frank's team a return to European football after an absence of eighteen years.

Kilmarnock's UEFA Europa League adventure was brief, they exited the competition in the first qualifying round, but Steve Clarke went on to manage the national team.

And, despite Scotland's abject, and often humiliating, failure on the international stage for a generation and more, and the fact that the job was considered to be a heavily poisoned chalice strapped to an improvised explosive device, he had mostly succeeded in defying his country's modest expectations.

Scotland now stood on the brink of qualification for their first appearance at a major tournament since FIFA 98 in France.

Euro 2020 would not in the end take place until 2021, but all that was yet to come. For now, Frank, and Peter Galbraith, and The Tartan Army were thoroughly looking forward to it.

# 3. Perfect

What little he knew about communications he had learned on the job. It was not a subject that he had ever studied. But in that, he was not unusual. Brussels functionaries were expected to be generalists. That is to say, they were not expected to know much about anything in particular.

He had been her client, albeit not one who could or was ever expected to express an opinion on her work, far less to pass judgement on it. The work of contractors was not something that was judged, or approved, or rejected, it was simply validated, or more often it was not.

Presentations to the European Parliament always took place at their buildings. And she was impressed by the trappings of power that they and their cavernous meeting rooms projected.

Today they were on the seventh floor of the Wilfried Martens Building on Rue Belliard, a new, and particularly well-appointed office, that Frank and his unit had only recently occupied.

It had been commissioned, Frank was told, to provide more and bigger meeting rooms, though Frank had kept any mention of the more obvious and cheaper alternative solution to himself.

He arrived late and noticed her immediately. As luck would have it the only remaining vacant chair in the room was next to hers. He sat down. She smiled.

He smelled of cigarettes, cigarettes and bergamot. For the next three hours, he said nothing, but as the meeting approached its inconclusive conclusion, and began to dissolve into small talk, he slid his card along the table to her: "Pleased to meet you" he said, and he rose to his feet.

He shook her hand firmly, but at the same time gently. His smile was warm, she thought. He looked at his shoes for what seemed to her to be an eternity, and then he left the room.

Alone on the terrace, he lit a cigarette. English? No, her accent was too good for her to be English. And she didn't have English skin. She had perfect skin. A song from his student days in Glasgow played in his head. She was a contractor, so he could call her. But what was her name? He could find out but news of such an enquiry would undoubtedly not take long to reach Renaud's ears. Renaud? Where was Renaud? He was not here.

He had not been in the meeting. Or had he? Frank realised that he could not now remember if Renaud had been there or not. He could not now remember the work, or even what the meeting had been about. No matter, its conclusion would have been that there would be another meeting.

The following evening, at home, Frank was surprised, but not displeased, to find her still in his head, and all the more so when she messaged him.

He waited forty minutes or so, while, for the first time in a long time, he listened to the whole of that first Lloyd Cole record again from start to finish. Then, unable to wait a moment longer, he accepted her invitation to lunch.

He added an x, deleted it, and pressed send.

# 4. Ste. Catherine

Fiona woke early, surprised to find herself excited by the prospect of her date.

The sun shone through the gaps in the slatted wooden blinds in the bedroom. She got up and made herself a coffee. She took it out to the terrace and she lit a cigarette.

It had been six years since she and Geert and Gabriel had moved to Brussels, four since she and Geert had separated, and only a matter of months since the divorce.

She had not dated seriously in all that time. She had not felt ready and there had been no-one who had caught her eye as Geert had once done and as Frank had done now.

She stripped the bed and remade it fresh. And then she showered and dressed.

In Brussels she had reverted to the style that she had favoured as a student in Peckham before Geert had transplanted her to North London and begun his doomed attempt to fashion her into a wife and a mother.

She put on the black calf-length leather skirt and the white silk blouse that she had collected from the dry cleaners yesterday, the newest of her three pairs of black ankle boots, and her vintage Levis jacket, bought in a second hand store in Beacon Hill that last summer she lived there.

Though her invitation to Frank might have appeared impulsive, it was again more intuitive. Once more not so much the bravura of knowing that she could invite him, and that he would accept the invitation, but a question of why not, as much as why?

She knew nothing about him, except for the certain fact that he would be her lover. She had known it about Geert, and now she knew it about Frank. But she had not, so far as she could now recall, ever known it about anyone else.

The Noordzee was a bar and grill attached to a fish shop on the corner of Place Ste. Catherine and Rue de Flandre, no more than a ten minute walk from her apartment.

There were no seats, customers either stood at the bar or else at the high tables arranged under umbrellas on the Place Ste.Catherine.

Frank was already well installed, drinking a glass of Sauvignon Blanc and smoking a cigarette, when Fiona arrived, only an entirely acceptable fifteen minutes late. If he was at all nervous, which he was, then she could detect no sign of it.

She surprised him by taking his arm and kissing him on the cheek, inhaling slightly as she did so, he thought, though he could have been wrong, or else she might have had a cold.

"May I?" she said politely, taking a cigarette from his packet. "You may" he answered. Frank lit it for her. And they laughed, and they began to talk about the English language and English people and about what had brought them both to Brussels and why.

She took a glass of the Sauvignon Blanc and then agreed that they should share a bottle. They ordered a dozen oysters, which they shared, and then a tuna steak which Fiona toyed with before feeding most of it to Frank with her fork.

She told him about growing up in Seattle with her mother, and he told her about growing up in Irvine without his.

She told him about Geert and about Gabriel, and he told her about the Dutch girl.

A second bottle of wine arrived without Frank noticing that Fiona had ordered it, and a bottle of petillante, and then more food; shrimp croquettes, and fried scampi.

"English?" the server asked Frank, presumably enquiring as to his nationality as his native language was surely already apparent. "Scottish" Fiona answered for Frank with what he thought sounded like something almost approaching pride.

And both, now a little drunk, found this funny.

It began to rain. Frank settled the bill. He told Fiona that he could not under any circumstances accept hospitality from a contractor.

Which was true, but which again, seemed to them to be amusing. Fiona took an umbrella from her shoulder bag, opened it, and held it over Frank's head.

She kissed him, on his other cheek this time, and then again very gently on the lips. Belgian kissing protocol was complex, Frank knew, but again, this surprised him.

He tasted her cigarette, and the tip of her tongue. He felt a little dizzy, but that would likely be the Sauvignon Blanc. Suddenly the rain was heavy.

It bounced off the cobblestones as they crossed Place Ste.Catherine. She took his arm. "Let's walk," she said,"and get a coffee."

The walk was brief. The sign above the door said: 'The Daringman' but the bar in which Frank now found himself seated had long ago become synonymous with its proprietor, and was known, and well known, in the quarter, simply as 'Chez Martine'.

The room was small and narrow, with a red Formica topped bar running most of the width of the back wall. Wooden bench seating ran down both sides of its length. Red Formica topped tables and wooden chairs stood opposite, leaving the corridor between them at best a metre wide.

A bar, Frank thought, from a Tom Waits song, or an Edward Hopper painting.

Fiona returned with a wooden tray. Two expressos, two small glasses of water, two speculoos biscuits, two coffee spoons, two sugars, and two cognacs.

She squeezed herself around the table and slid up the bench until not a millimetre separated them. She put her hand on Frank's thigh."Why does everyone think you're English?

Frank looked up to see the barman looking at him. He nodded and smiled. "The cognac was his idea, I guess he thought you might be needing it."

"To be fair, I thought that you were English at first" he said. Fiona half laughed "if only."

She seemed to know the local barmen well, not that that, in Frank's eyes, was necessarily any bad thing. But did any of them know her?

He woke to the sound of distant church bells, naked and alone in the fresh white cotton sheets of Fiona's bed, six, seven, eight, nine, ten. There may have been more, he was unsure.

His pants, his trousers and his shirt lay over a tattered armchair that stood in the corner of the room. He got up and dressed. He heard a key turn in a lock in the room beyond and went to find her. She put the bread and the orange juice down on the kitchen table and kissed him.

And he kissed her. And the two of them kissed each other as though both were connected to the same shared ventilator.

She unbuttoned his shirt and unbuckled his belt, she undid her jean shorts and they fell to the wooden floor. She turned around and rested her hands on the slate worktop.

And wearing her ankle boots and what she had described, only yesterday, as her minimal underwear, she brought all the enthusiasm of last night's lovemaking to this morning's fucking.

She seemed to be in more of a hurry this morning.

She turned to face him, and they kissed again. She lit a cigarette and passed it to him. He sat down on a red upholstered chrome barstool that seemed familiar to him from somewhere.

He watched her cook as he smoked his cigarette and drank his coffee.

13

They ate scrambled eggs on buttered toast with smoked salmon, lemon juice and pepper. They drank orange juice.

And neither of them now feeling very much in need of any words, they did so in silence.

Frank could not recall eating anything since yesterday's oysters and tuna and shrimps and scampi. He felt contentment fill his stomach.

It spread to his thoughts and finally settled in his heart.

"Geert will bring Gabriel over at four," she said. "It's his week here, I must tidy up this life, and become mum. And you must tidy up yours, and become whoever it is that you are".

'Whoever it is that you are.' The turn of phrase struck him as odd, but he said nothing.

# 5. Somewhere Else Entirely

He took the Metro from Ste. Catherine to Schumann, and then walked for a minute or so around the corner to the Bus Stop on Rue Archimede.

He walked past the barricades and the barbed wire, and the army trucks, and the soldiers, bored after what was now nearly nine months on the streets, without really noticing any of it.

A banner hung the height of the corner of the Berlemont Building that faced him: 'The Junker Commission. Working For EU' it said in bold italic English, French, Dutch, and twenty-one more languages, all above an enormous European Flag.

It had hung here for as long as Frank could remember and he had, on more than one occasion, described it to colleagues as looking like something that had been written by a speak your weight machine and designed by a colour-blind Mexican on acid, wearing gloves.

But that sunny Sunday afternoon in June, he didn't give it either a second glance or a moment's thought. Nor did he notice that the Sunday service of the Number 60 was so infrequent that he had been standing there for almost forty minutes before one finally arrived.

Frank McDonald, whoever he was, was in love with Fiona Anderson whoever she was. And for today that was all that he wished to focus on. The knowledge that it is those who do not know who they are that present the greatest danger would come, but for now it could wait.

He got off the bus at Le Poutre and navigated his way past the well-groomed children of the well-groomed families taking their long Sunday brunches on the corner terrace of The Toucan Brasserie.

Normally just the sight of these people would have annoyed him intensely, if irrationally. But today was not normal. Today it seemed to cheer him. He caught the eye of a small boy drawing on a napkin and he bid him a cheerful "Bon Appetit"

He crossed the road to his apartment, took his keys from his pocket, clicked the key fob, and pushed open the heavy wrought iron door to the building. The elevator door closed behind him. He checked his eyes in the mirror. He was not among the undead yet, in fact, this afternoon he felt very much alive, if perhaps a little tired.

Inside the apartment the lights were on. Yesterday, when he had left, though he may have hoped, he had not expected that he would be out for long.

He placed his phone, his keys, and his wallet on the dining table, took a shower and changed. He lay down on the sofa, placed two pillows behind his head, and turned on the TV.

Aside from the Champions League, The Andrew Marr Show was pretty much the only programme that Frank ever watched regularly. The Scottish Premier League was not offered by any so-called service provider in the building. He had long given up hope of ever being able to watch any Kilmarnock game anywhere.

It was the only programme that he ever recorded. Not on account of any particular lingering interest in British politics, but because he had always liked its host.

Andrew Marr was a fellow countryman and a fellow historian, who, although ten years his senior, Frank felt as though he had grown up with. He had what Scots like to describe as a forensic mind and he was, for Frank at any rate, one of the few remaining people on television who could still be considered to be, in any meaningful sense of the word, a journalist.

He had yet no way of knowing it, but that day, Sunday, June 19th 2016, would mark the start of a week that would change everything that Frank knew. Though not quite as much as the woman he had spent the night with. But that was all yet to come.

Interviewed by Marr, David Cameron looked relaxed and sounded confident, but this was a man who never looked anything but relaxed and never sounded anything but confident. That was just what he did, and, as it was soon to turn out, that was just about all he did.

But there were few who would have put their own money on him being gone within the week. And Frank was not among them.

Next was Boris Johnstone, Cameron's Court Jester, and until recently his friend and colleague. He had been grilled by Marr last week, and had made a fool of himself.

But there were few who would have put their own money on him eventually succeeding Cameron. And Frank was not among them.

But that, and many stranger things, were soon to come.

Today there was a clip of Boris, he was always Boris and never Johnstone, far less Mr Johnstone, a chummy man of the people name for the chummy man of the people persona that he had so carefully spun. He was emerging from a bus, a perennially popular motif of British Politicians, in the car park of some grimly anonymous suburban office park. It was a red bus, and painted along its side was the promise that Britain's entire annual

EU budget would be used instead to fund The National Health Service, a cherished, indeed a sacred, British institution.

If only, and here's the rub, the country was to vote Leave.

The sum of money was unbelievable. But there were few who would have put a pound of it on that being the outcome. And Frank was not among them.

He yawned and stretched and adjusted his head on the pillows. At least it would all be over by the end of the week, he told himself. There had been no need for any of it in the first place, but at least this would settle it now, once and for all.

And so reassured, Frank thought of Fiona, at first sexually, and then romantically, and then briefly maternally, with her son, as he drifted into a deep contented sleep.

He would often nap here for anything between forty-five minutes and a couple of hours. But although it was still light outside, it was four hours later, and gone nine o'clock, before he woke.

He lay for a moment, regaining his bearings, and gathering his thoughts, before he got up. He picked up his phone from the table and connected it to the charger.

There were a hundred and twenty-three unread emails, but most of these were from the last time that he looked on Friday afternoon. They could wait for another day. Most, in fact, could wait for another week, or another month.

There were three WhatsApp messages from his neurotic Spanish neighbour, Pepa. But as none of them concerned mice, nor electricity, nor the gas supply, and were, rather, only two enquiries as to his whereabouts, and a vague invitation to supper, he also left them unanswered.

There was no message from Fiona, and so, rather than choose to interrupt her, instead he read her invitation to lunch, and his reply, once again. And that contented him.

He removed the stopper from the already open bottle of Bruily that stood among its reinforcements on the kitchen sideboard and poured himself a large glass. He went to the fridge and took a glass of petillante. He took both back to the sofa and turned on the TV again.

Michael Palin was trekking in India. It was a programme that he had seen before. And, although he held Michael Palin in almost as high regard as Andrew Marr, India was not a place that had previously interested him.

His Grandfather, on his mother's side, had served as an army officer there, but Frank had never met him and there was no family history of him that he had ever heard.

Frank had never been nor ever really entertained any thought of going. Nor had he shared his Father's enthusiasm for Indian food. But through the lens of love the place seemed to reveal its beauty and wisdom to him and he found himself fascinated.

There was a military parade. Marching soldiers spun like dancers. Flags were lowered.

He drank his wine, and he sipped his water, and he lit a cigarette. There was bagpipes playing. He thought of Ayrshire, and Scotland, and his father, and Fiona. He was slightly drunk.

He brushed his teeth, undressed, and went to bed. And, despite the hours he had already slept, he fell quickly back into deep sleep once more.

And soon, in his dreams, he was in India.

He was watching flags being lowered. There were bagpipes. He was with Michael Palin, only Michael Palin wasn't Michael Palin, he was Fiona.

A message appeared silently on the phone beside his bed as he slept, sweet dreams, my love, it said. And it was signed with an x.

# 6. The Leper

Renaud dressed, in Frank's opinion, as though he were taking his dog for a walk.

He was not scruffy, quite the opposite, it was just that he seemed to have no other wardrobe than smart casual. There was surely no other place on earth where men habitually wore red corduroy trousers.

His short thinning hair was permanently gelled, a vanity that Frank thought pointless. He was a metre shorter than Frank and held no higher qualification than a Bachelor's Degree in Media Studies from a polytechnic in Liege.

He considered Frank, as an Anglo-Saxon, genetically incapable of being a European.

And yet there had always seemed to be something else between them, something deeper. Something that Frank could never quite put his finger on that he always felt when he found himself in his company, which was something that he tried to avoid whenever he could.

As it would turn out the feeling was well founded. And when the day of its discovery came, it would shock him deeply, though it should not have surprised him at all.

Renaud enjoyed more influence, led a larger department, commanded a bigger budget, and, crucially, had, or seemed to have, the ear of the Director.

He was evangelical about all things social and digital. Frank was not. Preferring to maintain a healthy scepticism of what he liked to refer to as their vanity metrics and the free pass afforded to their proprietors to mark their own homework.

Besides, Facebook and Google were not European either, nor genetically capable of ever being so. And was it not a little disingenuous, if not entirely hypocritical, for a liberal democracy to pour its money into unaccountable American tech monopolies whose every act seemed calculated to undermine liberty and democracy?

Whatever the intellectual merit of his position, Frank was in a minority in holding it, and pretty much entirely on his own in expressing it. That train had left the station, and Renaud and his fundamentalists held sway. Frank certainly did nothing to persuade anyone of the contrary by openly referring to them as The Taliban. A joke that would eventually turn out to be even more grimly inappropriate than he thought at the time.

That was not to say that Frank did not enjoy the occasional victory, or at least the odd score draw. Renaud was powerful, but he was not popular.

He was overconfident, and often overbearing. He had a reputation for sucking up to those above him while shafting those beneath him. He could be, some said, his own worst enemy. Though not, as Frank was fond of adding, while Frank still had breath in his body.

Frank's political colour, though undeclared and not easily discerned, was a matter of suspicion among his colleagues, and, more importantly, his superiors. Although always outwardly obedient to the compromises by which European Politics advance, he was no conservative.

As an undergraduate he had flirted with Scottish Nationalism. And although he thought that he had finally come down on the 'Yes' side of the argument in The Independence Referendum, on the day he wavered, and ended up marking his cross in the 'No' box.

In that, he was not alone among pro-European Scots of his generation.

He distrusted the flags and the anthems that were the Nationalist's and Renaud's stock in trade. Further proof that Frank was just another priest who did not believe in God.

Frank had felt that his 'coat was on a shoogly peg' as his father might have put it, long before Brexit, but the truth was a good deal more nuanced. Whilst it was always possible that he might end up in some form of internal exile, archiving in Luxembourg, for example, he knew it was all but impossible to lose his job.

Or was it? It was not long before the story began to circulate that if British Citizens were no longer to enjoy the right of residence in Belgium then they would no longer be able to fulfil the terms of their contracts of employment. If the story did not originate with Renaud then he was certainly doing his best to spread it.

No, Frank would not lose his job, but he may no longer be able to perform it, same difference.

He put this thought to the back of his mind.

In those early days, the smart money in Brussels did not believe that the British would ever leave. They would have second thoughts. They would change their minds. As the Danish had done, and the Irish. Or else the Germans would change their minds for them.

In London too, as the Remainers woke up to the scale of the ineptitude of their campaign, if not yet their arrogance, the feeling, or the hope, at least, was that there would be a second vote, a 'people's vote' and everything would be all right in the end.

And if it was not then, there would no doubt be some sort of a fix for the status of Frank and those like him. Anyway, it would all take years to reach any sort of a conclusion.

Years in which Frank would continue to sit in meetings feigning interest in discussions about what is, and what is not, heteronormative imagery.

A man and a woman strolling hand in hand on a beach, he would learn to his surprise, is, and should not be used to communicate with citizens in any circumstances, even if the man and the woman in question, as Frank had suggested, purely for the sake of argument, are siblings.

Discussions about how best to communicate integration, or was it diversity, or was it both, it was all so complicated now that he could no longer remember. A disabled, or rather, differently-abled, person must always be depicted in the company of an abled person apparently, otherwise the communication might suggest exclusion.

Discussions during which he would be told: "You just can't say that about freedom of speech." That at least was funny, but as day followed day, and absurdity piled upon absurdity, he began to find himself less and less able to see the joke in any of it.

Perhaps the British would leave. Perhaps he would leave. Perhaps that might not be such a bad thing after all. Perhaps there was a life after this, an afterlife. Perhaps that was the way he would yet come to avoid eternity walking amongst the undead.

Frank told himself to relax, which, despite the possibility that that was what The Taliban wanted him to do, he mostly managed.

There was the rest of Euro 2016 to enjoy for one thing. And there was Fiona.

And so that summer, football and Fiona managed to occupy most of Frank's attention, and pretty much all of his time. A peaceful time. A more peaceful time, it seemed to him, than he had spent since, he tried to think, but no comparison came to mind.

Apart from his father, Frank had no family that he knew of, but he had never been short of friends. A leper at work perhaps, but one that had always been adept at changing its spots to whatever its social habitat demanded.

Had any of his colleagues ever taken the trouble, which they had not, they would have found that his world-weary sarcasm was a mask worn for their benefit. And that beneath it lay a kind heart and a generous soul.

No qualification or training as a therapist was needed to see the abandonment issues that festered, or to feel the rawness of the scars that remained unhealed. But the fact remained that, perhaps by some way of compensation for his suffering, he also possessed a considerable charm.

His facility with languages was a card that he played to his advantage. And even among those without any interest in football, his encyclopaedic knowledge of it was another string to his bow.

He was considered quick-witted and funny. Women felt relaxed in his company. He was handsome, but unselfconsciously so, well-groomed and well dressed, well-read and well-travelled, a talker for sure, but a listener also. He was generous, he was smart, and he was Scottish.

There was nothing whatsoever in his life experience that suggested, far less implied, the notion that any woman should ever be expected to care for him. Or that anything should necessarily be expected of her either, whoever she was.

One advantage of never really having had a mother was that he was certainly no mother's boy.

And yet there was no machismo about him either. He had, as a younger man, sometimes been taken for a homosexual. A fact that he liked to mention to women, always knowing that adding 'though never actually by a homosexual' would pretty much guarantee a laugh.

Frank liked laughter. It was a sound that had been absent from his childhood and now that he was able to, he encouraged it as often as he could.

He had certainly never wanted for female company. Although he did sometimes wish that he might have had more say in the choice of those that he had ended up on intimate terms with.

The Dutch girl was a case in point. Had he exercised a little more caution when they first met, he could have easily discovered that not only was her third husband still very much alive, but that he was also serving a fifteen-year sentence for armed robbery.

And that she herself held a conviction for unlawful possession of firearms, albeit one that was, as she frequently repeated, now spent.

In the end, nothing worse than tomato soup, or had it been hot water all along, had been spilt, but somewhere in his head, if not in his heart, Frank knew that he had had a lucky escape.

That the only thing he had retained from the experience was an occasional, and highly selective, memory of the sex, was significant. And something that still lingered as an issue in the continuing cycle of his serial monogamy. Undeniably powerful as his charm was, it was also entirely indiscriminate. And when added to equal parts insatiable need of affection, and incurable romanticism, all too often it proved to be a powerful, and in the case of the Dutch girl, an almost lethal, cocktail.

# 7. An Habitue

For all of the twenty-two years that Frank had spent in Brussels, he had lived in Ixelles. At first on the Place de Londres in The European Quarter, Gotham City as it was known to the locals, and then progressively further away from the comforting orbit of the mothership.

He moved first to Flagey, to a small apartment by the lake, and then to a larger place on Rue Tenbosch, where had had now lived for almost twelve years.

His gradual southerly progress reflected the regular salary increments that his rise through the ranks merited. And his diminishing fear of, if not quite growing confidence in, day to day life in the city that he had come to accept was, in the absence of any other, his home.

This part of Ixelles was a popular choice among those who could afford it. A good deal more expensive than the neighbouring communes of St. Gilles or Forest, it was, as a consequence, a good deal quieter, and a good deal safer.

People who need to get up early to go to work, or to take the children to school, after all, are not generally those who are up late at night disturbing others.

There was the Bois de La Cambre to walk, cycle, or horse-ride in, none of which Frank had ever even thought of doing. Or else to picnic in, which on Summer afternoons, he liked to do both regularly with friends, and frequently, on dates.

Closer to hand, at the end of his street, there was also the Parc Tenbosch, where he often took a lait russe, and a croissant from Kaiser, the French Patisserie on the corner of Bascule, to enjoy in the morning sun before going to work.

It was small and secluded, more a botanical garden than a proper park, and apart from the early morning dog walkers and the pre-school children and their nannies, rarely their mothers, this was Ixelles after all, it was quiet.

It was close to the European Institutions but not too close. There were shops, not all of which were all yet artisanal, or bio, or both. Some of them even still answered common everyday needs, like hairdressing and dry-cleaning.

Cafes and restaurants offered practically every form of carnivorous, pescatarian, vegetarian, and vegan cuisine known to humankind: Argentinian, Belgian, Chinese, French, Indian, Japanese, Korean, Lebanese, Nepalese, Mexican, Portuguese, Spanish, Thai and Turkish.

And yet the streets still thronged with Ubereats and Deliveroos ferrying what could not be found within walking distance to those too busy, too important, or simply too idle, to leave the house.

Or perhaps, as Frank often thought, they were in reality, mostly just ferrying McDonald's, Burger Kings, and KFCs to those too ashamed or too hypocritical to ever be seen to visit such places.

There were more, and certainly more expensive, opticians than any community, even one in which myopic Eurocrats were so heavily overrepresented, could ever need.

And a good deal more hairdressers than Frank thought necessary.

Frank had always appreciated the importance of a good haircut at least once a month. For one thing, he found that it always lightened his mood. And although the proprietor of the one that he frequented had eventually revealed himself to hold deeply racist and virulently anti-immigrant views, Frank continued to go there.

He was a good hairdresser, and maybe Frank should not have been in such a hurry to tell him what he did and where he worked.

What there was not was a bar to rival Chez Martine, or Au Laboreur, the location of his second date with Fiona and the setting of many more close encounters with her since.

There was Chez Franz which was pleasant enough, if rather too young, rather too French, and at weekends certainly, rather too busy, and rather too staffed by adolescent Renauds, for his taste.

And there was Cote d'Ivoire which, although outwardly appearing to be a more typical working man's Belgian Bar, revealed itself to be as a close to an identical replica of an 80's Disco in Magaluf as made no difference the moment you walked through the door.

In any event, despite his regular attendance and best efforts in both, Frank had never succeeded in becoming a true habitué in either. Perhaps nobody ever did.

Perhaps that was simply down to the fact that in Ixelles Eurocrats were a dime a dozen, whilst downtown they were, then at least, still something of a rarity. Albeit one that was far from universally popular.

Perhaps it was the football, perhaps it was his indiscriminate charm or his facility with languages, or perhaps it was just the fact that Frank's first introduction there was always as Fiona's boyfriend, but as summer turned to autumn, and then, as Brussels' brief autumn more quickly became winter, it was in Fiona's bars that his friendship circle began to widen.

It was not that Ste. Catherine was any more cosmopolitan than Ixelles, indeed in the number and variety of languages heard on the streets it was probably rather less so. But it went to bed later and it got up later, and on Fridays and Saturdays it barely seemed to need to go to bed at all.

It had a rougher edge and Frank quickly found himself at home there. It was, in many ways, a little of the walk on the wild side that Brussels had seemed to promise from afar but had, with the notable exception of the Dutch girl, so far failed to deliver.

If Ixelles was Edinburgh in all of its gentility, he thought, then Ste. Catherine was Glasgow in all of its honesty. There was certainly something of Glasgow's warmth to be found in the indiscriminate embrace of all of those who walked through the doors of Chez Martine and Au Laboureur. The latter stood on the corner of the Rue de Flandre and the Rue Leon Lepage, and although Fiona favoured the more intimate, and often younger and rather hipper, Chez Martine, to Frank, Au Laboureur suggested nothing so much as an idealised version of his student days in Glasgow.

Were it not for the large windows affording a view of the comings and goings on the crossroads beyond, and its extensive, though unheated, terrace, the proprietor, was careful with the warmth of his welcome in winter, Au Laboureur would not have looked out of place on Byres Road. Neither windows, large or small, nor terraces, of course, were much of a feature of Glasgow bars at the turn of the century, but the sight of the rain bouncing on cobblestones beneath the sulphurous yellow glow of ageing streetlights was reassuringly common to both.

As was the all-important, and omnipresent, sound of laughter.

The two bars were five minutes apart and entirely complimentary in their atmosphere. And Fiona and Frank together, as they now inseparably seemed to be, were not alone in sharing their company and custom in both.

Neither ever considered themselves ex-pats, but rather economic, and indeed cultural, migrants. That was to their credit, and they were not alone in it.

It was true that the majority of their ever wider, and ever deeper, friendship group here were Belgians, and many of them Dutch-speaking Belgians from Brussels. But there were also Algerian Belgians, Congolese Belgians, Italian Belgians, Moroccan Belgians, Senegalese Belgians and Yugoslavian Belgians among them too.

Conversations were conducted in English, Dutch, French, and Arabic,

25

depending on who was at the table, or who held the chair, or the floor, at the time, but snatches of Italian, Spanish, Portuguese or Polish were also to be heard.

What any of these people did for a living was unimportant, and often unknown, though among the circle of those that Fiona, at least, knew well, there was, to Frank's knowledge, an accountant, an academic, an actor, a builder, a courier, three graphic designers, an IT consultant, two musicians, a writer, a nurse, and a secretary, but not, to Frank's relief, one single social media strategist.

To say that this brought out the Scot in Frank was only a part of the truth. It also brought out the human and the humanitarian. The knowledge instilled at birth that whoever we are, and wherever we come from, we are all 'Jock Tamson's Bairns'.

It brought out the European in him. The European that the Anglo-Saxon blood in his veins meant that, in the eyes of Renaud at least, he could never be.

But was not this community, this organic, inclusive, supportive, tolerant, indiscriminate and undiscriminating community, this European community precisely what Frank and Renaud and the rest of their colleagues were supposed to be building?

And it bought out the romantic in him too, the true romantic. For was this not really, in Fiona's parting words to him on their first date 'whoever it is that you are.'

# 8. Ever Closer Union

By now it was clear to Fiona that her intuition had been entirely correct. She had known that since the first sight of him, the first sound of him, the first smell of him, the first touch of him, and the first taste of him.

More so than her intuition about Geert certainly, Frank had no need, nor any desire to fashion her into anything, least of all a wife or a mother.

Though the thought had occurred to her, more than once these last two years, that she could marry him, if she wished, and that, perhaps in time, she would.

And that there was still time yet for them to have a child together, a sister for Gabriel, why not? And yet, at the same time why? She was happy, he was happy. Life was good, why change it?

There was more than a grain of truth in Geert's words when they divorced. She was a woman, he said, who you could never be certain would always be yours, even if you were certain that you would always be hers. A woman whose only constant is change. She knew it herself, and she felt the first stirrings of it again now even as she and Frank drew closer.

It had been a simple thing for him to know that she was not English. And a simple thing for him to find that there was so much in their hearts that felt the same, and so much in their minds that thought the same.

And to take a simple joy in the immense and unfamiliar pleasure that brought him.

To believe that they had found each others missing half, by chance, one morning in a meeting room in the Wilfried Martens Building on Rue Belliard. To feel that they were alone together in the world. Charles Aznavour sang in his head, or was it Elvis Costello?

Of her hundred different things the most puzzling to Frank were her hundred different gurus.

That most were from California, or the Left Coast, as her mother liked to call it, was unsurprising. Most of them she had first found on her mother's bookshelves, and she had returned to them and to their teachings, and to those of the generation that had followed them, in London.

Many of them were also Indian, but that too was unsurprising. Although it had not yet really occurred to Frank that perhaps Fiona herself had some of the makings of a guru in her blood.

But he remembered what an Indian friend had once told him. Gurus are mostly an export line on the sub-continent. You don't find many Indians with very much time for them.

It was in London also that she had all but eliminated any trace of an American accent and in removing all but the last few tell-tale signs of an American English vocabulary.

She sounded less American than many of Frank's colleagues who had never set foot in the country. Those Hungarians and Poles who spoke of crosswalks and sidewalks. Those Romanians and Czechs who stressed the wrong syllable of garage.

Had Frank thought about it, the fact that she had managed to do this so thoroughly must have required some effort and not a little practice. But Frank did not think about it. Because thinking about it would have required that he exercised a degree of caution that he knew himself incapable of.

And in any case, Fiona was not a woman who invited caution, nor one who welcomed it. And in that, as in much else, they were well matched.

If women felt comfortable in his company, then men felt equally comfortable in hers.

Though some women sometimes did not. And though she had eyes only for Frank and no romantic interest in anyone else, she had been known to provoke jealousy among some of the more socially conservative wives and girlfriends in their friendship group.

She could, and perhaps should, have shared less about how satisfied she was in bed.

And yet, it seemed to Frank, that it was hypocritical, sexist even, if that was a word that would ever pass his lips, that even among this socially liberal and sexually liberated demimonde, the qualities that were found to be charming in a man like him, were considered to be predatory in a woman like her.

It was not his loyalty to her, nor even his love for her, that caused him to know that, and express it, but a sense of the ignorance and the injustice that lay beneath it. Though there were those who would instead just call him naïve.

Had they known them in the way that only they knew each other, then those who liked such certainty of judgement might have better understood that the childhood which had led Frank to expect nothing from women was no different to that which had led Fiona to expect nothing of men.

In both there was a hunger. A longing to be a part of something more.

To be anchored to someone, or something, or somewhere. A longing just to belong.

In Fiona it was satisfied, at least in part, by her gurus, and in Frank, by his football.

Frank had once heard it said that our identity is nothing more than who we are when nobody is looking, but he could not remember where or when.

It sounded much too smart to have ever come from any of his colleagues, so it was likely something that had been said by some consultant or other. Consultants being, as the joke in his DG had it, experts whose advice you pay to ignore.

He identified with Peter Galbraith as a staunch Kilmarnock supporter and a loyal foot soldier in the Tartan Army. He identified as a Scot and as a European. But, post-Brexit, he did not now identify as British.

Nor, of course, as a Eurocrat, even if in truth that is what he was, and that was what others saw him as. He and Fiona identified as a couple, and were seen by most as a good one, and by some as a perfect one.

Fiona was creative, she was a feminist, and she was a mother, but she could simply not imagine a time when nobody was looking. In her, the longing was deeper, and the hunger more acute. She fed it with Facebook and with Instagram. Frank disliked both and used neither. They reminded him, not so much of drug abuse, which was by now already a common comparison, but of something much darker and much closer to home.

The inciting incident of his mother's slow decline and final demise had been an eating disorder that had coincided, if not been triggered, by post-natal depression. It had first been ignored and then misdiagnosed. It was, the doctors had said at the time, a highly unusual, if not a unique case, certainly in the west of Scotland in the 1970s.

It was not a subject he had ever discussed with Fiona, nor likely ever would.

Certainly not, Frank thought, surprised to find that he could allow himself a little humour in such darkness, over the white linen tablecloths of the restaurants where they now preferred to spend more and more of their evenings a deux, sharing a mutual, and a hearty, appreciation of Carbonnade and Onglet Echalottes with a good Cote du Rhone, or Moules Frites and Cabillaud Roti, with a nice cold Pinot Blanc.

All, more often than not, bookended with a Coupe de Champagne to start with, and a Mousse au Chocolat, a coffee, and maybe a little pousse cafe to finish.

Feeding each other's hunger for company, for conversation, for laughter, and for love.

For as Fiona had been impressed by the trappings of power in the room where they first met, she was attracted by the comforts that Frank's position and salary afforded them both. She had been raised with them, after all, and she had, not so long ago, chosen to marry an investment banker.

And so, over time, as their second summer together passed, the centre of gravity of their relationship began to shift, geographically at first, and then, inevitably, in other ways too.

Weeks with Gabriel were still spent downtown, sometimes with Frank, and sometimes not. And although they continued to frequent au Laboreur and Chez Martine, Fiona did so less frequently.

Instead, she preferred to pass their weeks alone together in Ixelles, on the terraces of Plasch on Place Brugmann, or The Canterbury on Avenue de l'Hippodrome. Shopping in Chatelain and Avenue Louise or walking in the Bois de La Cambre or The Parc Tenbosch

Making love with Frank in his apartment on Rue Tenbosch as frequently as ever, as passionately as that first Sunday morning in the kitchen in Ste Catherine, but now more tenderly, and more lovingly too.

Almost as if nobody was looking.

## 9. Father And Son

It was a warm, still, Wednesday evening the following June, and Frank was at Fiona's.

She was in the kitchen, grating some parmesan, and about to put on some fresh pasta for the remaining Bolognese that she had made earlier for Gabriel.

Gabriel was slowly making his way to bed. He was in no hurry. He liked it when Frank was here. For one thing, his mother was much funnier, a good deal more relaxed, and much less strict with him. If Frank were not here now he would already have been in bed an hour or more ago.

Gabriel spoke French at school, and Dutch with his father, but English with his mother and Frank. Of the three, he preferred English. It was a lot easier. Frank was also a lot easier than Lies, his father's girlfriend.

He liked it when he could watch football with Frank and he liked it when Frank told him stories, and when they went to Au Laboureur.

He liked their friends. He didn't know his father's friends, nor Lies's, although she did seem to spend a great deal of time with them on her phone.

Frank set the table for dinner, and took a glass of red wine into the small garden at the back of the apartment, beyond Fiona's bedroom, their bedroom. He lit a cigarette.

It was a UK number, but not one he recognised, and so would not normally have taken the call, but somehow something told him to answer.

Tom was his father's neighbour and Frank recognised his voice immediately: "I'm sorry to have to tell you this, Frank."

Tom had been with him. He had suffered a heart attack, which the doctor, who had been making up a foursome with Tom and his brother Ian, as it happened, said had killed him instantly.

There was nothing that any of them could have done. They were only on the 9th hole too, but at least it had been a glorious day. Frank thanked Tom and apologised for ending the call before Tom could provide any more details of the game, or comment on his father's putting.

He would call him back tomorrow.

He stood for a moment, but no tears came to his eyes. He finished the last of the wine in his glass and he put out his cigarette in one of the oyster shells that served as Fiona's ashtrays.

In the kitchen, he refilled Fiona's glass first, and then his. He sat down at the table. "My father died this afternoon," he said.

She turned off the pasta, turned and looked into his eyes. She crossed the room and sat astride his lap, facing him. She put her arms around his neck. She pressed his head against her chest and held him tightly.

She began to cry. And as the tears rolled down her cheeks and onto Frank's head, he looked up at her, and his shoulders, and then his arms, and then his whole body, began to shake

"Let it out" she whispered, "let it out." And as she pressed his head tighter still against her chest, he let out a primal howl of grief. She felt the wetness of his tears on her breasts. And the quickening beat of his heart against her own. "I love you, Frank".

Gabriel appeared unseen in the kitchen doorway."Can you come and tell me a story?" he said.

## 10. The 19th Hole

Bill McDonald was born in Monkton, in Ayrshire, in 1946, the only son of an only son.

Frank liked to say that the family bloodline had always been a thin one. But at least that made the family tree a simple matter, it really being not much more than a sapling.

His father was a tenant farmer, as his father had been before him. He died of a stroke at the age of fifty-six. His mother was a farmer's wife. They led a simple, but not uncomfortable, life.

Bill left school at sixteen and took an apprenticeship in the drawing office of Scottish Aviation at Prestwick Airport, next door to the farm, where he worked for fifty-four years, only finally retiring on his seventieth birthday. He married Jean Brown, the drawing office secretary, and the only daughter of a police inspector and a nurse in1964, at the age of nineteen. They spent their honeymoon in Scarborough during the Glasgow Fair Fortnight that August. Bill was never much of a man for holidays, and never once took a single day more than those that were mandated by law.

Frank could recall only one family holiday with both his mother and father. It was also in Scarborough. He could have been no more than five or six years old. And the only reason that he recalled it at all was that some years later the hotel that they had stayed in fell off the cliff that it stood on and into the sea.

Frank was born nine months after the honeymoon, pretty much to the week, on the 1st of May 1965, a Saturday. The USSR launched the Luna 5 moon rocket that day. Bill played golf. And with an irony that can only be explained by coincidence, 'Mrs. Brown, You've Got A Lovely Daughter' by Herman's Hermits, topped the charts.

Their first family home was in Irvine, a terraced house on the same street as Jean's parents. The young couple travelled to work at Prestwick together, in the brief times that Jean was well, by bus, cars still being beyond the means of most working folk in those days.

After Jean's death, Bill moved to Troon, ostensibly to be closer to his work, but in reality to put some distance between him and the melancholy of the marital home.

And between him and his in-laws, who not only considered that Jean had

33

married beneath herself but who would always and forever hold Bill responsible for what they would never refer to as anything other than their daughter's 'unhappiness'.

He bought a small, semi-detached, red sandstone bungalow on Harling Drive. It stood overlooking the eighteenth green of The Dalry, the longest, and the most challenging, of the town's three municipal golf courses, opposite the clubhouse that served them.

The funeral was, to Frank's surprise, well attended.

And the wake, held in the clubhouse bar, particularly so. Apart from Peter Galbraith, with whom Frank had drunk a bottle of Jura15 Year Old, his favourite single malt, the night before, Frank knew only half a dozen of the guests at best: Bill's neighbour Tom and his brother, Ian, their wives, Catherine and Sandy, and Doctor Livingstone.

For the most part, the others were Bill's former work colleagues or golfing partners. His in-laws, Frank's only remaining relatives, did not attend.

As he made his way around the room, politely accepting condolences, the truth began to dawn on him, that not only did he know nothing about his father's work, he knew even less about his life.

And he realised as he listened to them talk of his father, and talk of him warmly, that Bill had been a good man. And that his inability to have seen that, or even to have bothered to look, until now that it was too late, had not been down to his father, but to him.

A pang of guilt hit him. For was it not the truth that he had abandoned his father, just as his mother had abandoned him?

He felt Fiona squeeze his hand. She had arrived from Brussels this morning and would return tomorrow. Yet here she was at his side, offering him her love, as she offered ham and tomato sandwiches, scotch eggs, and pork pies, to a roomful of total strangers.

Talking with, and listening to, each of them as though they all regularly spent Friday nights together at Chez Martine, and had so done for years. Squeezing Frank's hand, kissing his cheek, and as the whisky flowed, to squeezing his butt and kissing his lips.

Something that did not escape the notice, nor the whispered disapproval, of more than one of the wives in the room. Nor the quiet envy of more than one of their husbands.

As the coffee and the shortbread was served, the room began to thin out, and the last of the mourners drifted home for their tea, Frank and Fiona slipped outside.

They sat together on the wooden bench by the 18th green. She lit a cigarette and handed it to him and then lit another for herself.

She took his hand, and they sat together for a moment in silence looking across the road at the house on Harling Drive.

The last of the golfers putted out the last of their games in the slowly setting sun of the longest day. "Why eighteen?" she said, and Frank laughed, and they kissed. She tasted of whisky and cigarettes, as did he, and they tasted good to each other.

"I have absolutely no idea at all," he said, " I guess that's something you'll need to ask Tom".

Tom and Catherine's front room was not used often. His father had a similar place with much the same lack of purpose. Most Scots of their generation did. It was not considered a pretension, but rather a deserved respect for the importance of certain days and certain rituals.

The front room was always kept for best, for Christmas Day, and New Year, for christenings and special birthdays, and now also, as Catherine was proud to point out, for funerals too. This being the first of many, she hoped, somewhat tactlessly.

She was drunk, all four of them were drunk, whisky drunk, and there was more to come. Tom's best single malt, a Talisker Twenty-Five Year Old, was opened.

Frank sipped his appreciatively, but slowly. He always knew when he had had enough. Fiona often did not. But tonight at least she had the good sense to add more water than was considered respectful, and then to pour most of her glass into Frank's while their hosts were distracted.

Fish and Chips appeared, and cakes. Determined not to let Frank down, Fiona did her best. But by the time Tom began a lengthy and detailed exposition of the origins and rules of The Royal And Ancient Golf Club of St. Andrews, she found herself no longer able to follow any of it.

She felt dizzy, and a little sick. In the taxi back to the hotel, she fell asleep in his arms. He carried her to the room, undressed her, and put her to bed. He drew the curtains and put out the light. It was still only ten o'clock, and there was still plenty of day left in the sky.

He went down to the bar and he took one last whisky, a large Jura, a Ten-Year-Old, which would just have to do, out onto the terrace.

The Marine had seen better days. The carpets were worn, the paint chipped, and the windows rotten, but it had once been one of Scotland's grandest hotels. In the1960s, Nikita Khrushchev stayed here, and Mick Jagger. And just about every golfer that anyone had ever heard of, as well as plenty more that no-one ever would.

That was back in the days when The Open Championship had been played over The Royal Troon, or The Old Troon as his father knew it. Not that he had ever played it. The Old Troon was not for working folk like Bill, but the bosses.

Frank woke to find Fiona freshly showered. And naked beside him, her head resting on his chest, her long black hair tied loosely. This morning she tasted of lemons and honey. And that song, which was her song now, and would never be anyone else's song, played again in his head.

She did not speak, she did not need to, the gentle smile that played on her lips and danced in her eyes said all that she needed to say and all that he wished to know.

She kissed his shoulder, and then his neck, he turned his head without lifting it from the pillow, and she flicked the tip of her tongue over his lips. They had both long agreed that morning lovemaking was generally better than evening lovemaking, that afternoon lovemaking was often better than either, and that hotel room lovemaking was always especially enjoyable, irrespective of the time of day.

That lovemaking was something that was possibly better enjoyed without, or at least before, the consumption of alcohol, was also something that had been discussed, but more concerning their level of alcohol consumption, rather than the quality, or frequency, of their lovemaking. Certainly, neither had ever had cause to complain that they had ever been anything but satisfied.

She clasped each of his hands tightly in each of hers and sat astride him, pulling him up towards her to press his head firmly against her breasts. She shook loose her hair.

And, reasoning correctly that Frank could not reasonably be expected to be at his best today, she made love to him, with all the strength in her perfect skin and all the passion in her perfect heart.

There was a knock on the door. "Coming," she said.

Frank pulled the sheets over his naked body. Fiona got up, pulled on a bathrobe, and answered the door. She signed Frank's name and came back to bed with the room service breakfast that she had ordered while he slept. There were some items among the Full Scottish Breakfast, or The Scottish Salad, as Frank liked to call it, that she was unfamiliar with. But Frank was happy to explain what he could, and to eat what she didn't like the sound of; the haggis, or the taste of; the Lorne sausage.

Both agreed though that the Tattie Scone, a fried pancake of potato and flour on which sat a fried egg, was just exactly what was needed this morning.

They showered together and they dressed. And then they took the path around the Royal Troon Clubhouse and walked along the South Beach to

36

the railway station.

Families picnicked in the dunes, children built sandcastles to stand against the tide, dog walkers walked their dogs, paddle boarders paddled their boards, and the occasional swimmer bobbed up and down in the sunlit surf.

It was not as Frank remembered it when he had partied here that last summer before university. The summer his mother died. Too shy then to even talk to girls, as he and his friends huddled around their bonfires, drinking warm cider, and passing the occasional illicit spliff among them in the chill evening air.

It was not as he remembered it at all, nothing was, it was all different now, and it was all better. Far, far better than anything that Frank could ever have imagined then.

Fiona took his arm. "I want us to come back here," she said, " I want us to bring Gabriel".

# 11. In My Father's House

There were many boxes. A few remained unpacked from the move from Irvine, thirty or more years ago, but most were more recent. Looking at them now it seemed to Frank as if Bill had been preparing the evidence of his life for storage, or disposal, even as he lived it.

Their contents were ordered with the meticulous care of the draftsman that he had been. And Frank began the task of working through them with the detachment of the historian that he was.

But no sooner he had begun to do so than he felt a change. This was a historical archive, and he was a historian, but the gravitational pull that he now felt was not that of academic curiosity.

He felt the same pang of guilt that he had felt yesterday, but it was sharper and more physical. A pain in his chest, a shortage of breath, his hands felt cold as he squatted, then knelt, and then finally sat on the patterned living room carpet.

At first sight, there did not appear to be anything of Bill's childhood. There were a few pictures of Jean as a young woman, but there were no wedding photographs, nor any evidence that he had ever been married. There were some of Frank's school reports, and a couple of his school photographs, some newspaper cuttings reporting Frank's later academic achievements, and others recording Bill's victories in Golf Tournaments.

But almost everything else seemed to be related to Bill's work. More newspaper cuttings announced orders for aeroplanes, or else their delivery. There were photographs of Bill among his colleagues and his bosses, with Margaret Thatcher, with The Queen, with suited American airline executives, one of whom Frank recognised had once been an astronaut, with a group of uniformed African airforce officers, and with all sorts of other people, all less identifiable.

In most of the photographs, there was an aeroplane, sometimes there were two or three. In several, Bill was front and centre of the action. In some, he was smiling, and in one or two he was laughing. Something Frank had never seen, nor ever heard. There were letters of appreciation and thanks. There were company memos announcing staff promotions and retirements.

And there were dozens and dozens of pens and pencils and erasers.

There were bottles of ink. There were boxes of tacks and pins. There were T-squares, triangles, dividers, protractors, rulers and compasses. Not that Frank, who had never shown much interest or ability in Mathematics, had any idea of which was which.

There were slide rules. And there were rolls and rolls and rolls of drawings. Drawings of such intricacy and perfection that, had they not been parts of aeroplanes, might have been mistaken for natural forms, birds, perhaps.

Drawings of the quality of Renaissance anatomical studies, the work of Albrecht Durer maybe, but they were not. All were drawn in the later years of the twentieth century before computers were capable of such things, and all were the work of Bill McDonald,

Each was signed as such by 'William McDonald, Draftsman' then in later years by 'William McDonald, Chief Draftsman' and then, more recently by 'William McDonald, Drawing Office Manager.'

Each one, not only an exact two-dimensional representation of the shape and dimensions of the part of the wing, or the rudder, or the wheel, or the door, or the window of the aeroplane, but the precise specification of its material, its finish and its tolerances.

Each, an original, to be copied and circulated to the machinists on the factory floor and the fitters on the assembly line. To be studiously followed in the manufacture of the aeroplane.

And then, passed on to the engineers in Chicago or Dallas, or Accra or Nairobi, who would be responsible for its upkeep and maintenance.

Each was both a map and also a narrative, practical and instructive like the Bill that Frank had never known. And yet, at the same time, creative and communicative like, well, like the woman who had made love to him this morning.

And, as Frank sat among it all, humbled as the child he could no longer be, in the presence of the father who was no longer there, he thought of Fiona, and he wondered why he had never thought to bring her here to meet his father.

He wondered what she would have made of him, and what he would have made of her. And to his surprise, he concluded that they would most likely have got along well.

And he thought it likely that he would have got along with her father, the aerospace engineer. It was a small world, right enough, and all the smaller for aeroplanes and those who made them.

The thought comforted him, and seemed for a moment, in his imagination, to somehow draw all of them closer though they had never met, and never would.

And he realised then that Bill had not ordered the evidence of his life for storage or disposal.

But that he had taken considerable time, and no small effort, to edit and curate it. In the patient, certain knowledge that this day would come. The day that Frank would sit here, and come to understand his life and what it meant to him. To appreciate it, and, perhaps, even to value it.

Frank looked down at a photograph of Bill laughing with his colleagues, and he thought: 'the old bugger' and then Frank laughed too.

It was now past eleven o'clock and it was almost dark outside. He went into the garden and lit a cigarette. He was tired from squatting and kneeling, and sitting on the floor. And he had just spent twelve hours sharing fifty-four years with the father who this morning he had barely known.

He found some pasta, a tin of tomatoes and a bottle of olive oil in the kitchen cupboard, and some parmesan in the fridge. He ate, and he made up a bed in the spare room.

He closed his eyes, but no dream came to him, or if it did, then no memory of it remained by morning. Instead, there were only his reflections on a dawning reality. It was too soon for Frank to begin to calibrate it. In the coming days and weeks, it would grow and its shape would change.

As the nature and purpose of his father's life inevitably forced comparison with his own.

## 12. A Bit Of A Mess

Frank woke, momentarily uncertain of where he was, and alarmed to find that Fiona was not beside him. He got up and dressed, for once in his life without showering or shaving, and he walked into town.

He bought a packet of cigarettes from the newsagent on the corner of Academy Street. And, for the first time in a long time, a newspaper. There was something still to be said for ink on paper after all, and plenty still for it to say, especially today.

He settled at the one unoccupied table on the terrace of The Tides Cafe, among the town's young families and its weekend visitors, and he ordered a latte and a bacon roll.

It was a pleasant enough day, though the temperature had dropped since Fiona had left. Those around him were sensibly dressed against the cold in anoraks and jumpers. They carried umbrellas. Scots knowing, like Scandinavians, that there is no such thing as bad weather, only inappropriate clothing.

A chill wind was already blowing in from The Firth of Clyde, bringing with it what any local knew would only be the first of the day's steady parade of rain clouds from The Atlantic beyond. The wind fluttered the faded, tattered Union Jack that flew from the Walker Hall across the street and the newer, cleaner, brighter, Saltire, beside it.

An aeroplane appeared in the distance, a speck at first among the clouds. Frank watched it as it grew larger and louder, descending over the deserted beach. Beneath its nose, and on either side of its belly, doors opened, and its wheels dropped into position.

He followed it until it disappeared beneath the rooftops and the tree line, lost in the moment as his childlike curiosity as to what it was, where it had come from, and where it was going, soured into frustration at his ignorance of these things.

By now, the aeroplane, a C-17 Globemaster of The United States Air Force, would be safely on the ground, taxiing past Bill's old drawing office to park up on the North Apron where it would be refuelled and its crew would rest.

It had come from Charleston, North Carolina, and was on its way to Rammstein in Germany, and then on to Bagram Airbase in Afghanistan.

But, of course, Bill would have known all that. Scottish Aviation had built parts for its predecessor, the Hercules, and Bill himself had first cut his teeth as an apprentice on its undercarriage assembly.

Frank sipped his coffee and ate his bacon roll. And he read The Herald. The paper that Bill had always taken and that he had always known as The Glasgow Herald. The paper that he had read as a student at Glasgow University and that he still read from time to time online in Brussels. It was good on Scottish Football, much better certainly than The Scotsman, its Edinburgh rival.

Its journalists regularly won awards, and its diary was still avidly read, or so it was said, by Sean Connery. But although considered, in the west of Scotland at least, to be the country's national newspaper, it was by no means a nationalist newspaper. In the Independence Referendum, it had supported Better Together and campaigned in favour of a No vote.

But much had changed in Scotland, and elsewhere, in the four years since then. Today's front page, like yesterdays, and tomorrow's too, led with Brexit. It was the second anniversary of the Referendum, and, that afternoon, a hundred thousand people would take to the streets of London in A People's March for a People's Vote.

Jeremy Corbyn, the leader of the Labour Party, would not be among them. And the People's Vote would, in any case, turn out to be red herring, and a dead one at that.

Frank turned the Herald's pages with a heavy heart. A large part of the argument advanced by Better Together, or Bitter Together, as it had been dubbed at the time, was that an Independent Scotland would have no hope whatsoever of being admitted to the European Union in the foreseeable future, if ever.

Europe had enough to worry about with its own separatists, as Frank's colleagues liked to call them, in Catalonia, not to mention Corsica or even Belgium. And then, of course, there were the two Cypruses. Not to mention the two Irelands, well, not for now, anyway.

Brussels had therefore chosen, with characteristic cowardice, Frank thought, not to get involved in the Brexit debate at all. Obama had made his views known, and had been pretty much universally criticised for doing so.

And, as was now beginning to become apparent, the Russians had also made their influence felt, though not openly, nor transparently, of course. Preferring to channel their dark money into social media posts about the hordes of immigrants waiting to flood England from across the sea.

In Frank's mind, that June morning, as he finished the last few crumbs of his bacon roll, there now seemed to be three equally interdependent, and equally intractable, problems.

For the British, it seemed that two years after voting for Brexit, there was nobody who knew what it meant or could describe what it might look like in practice. With every passing week, foreshadowing other, graver things from elsewhere that would not now be long in coming, Brexit seemed to mutate, into new and hitherto undiagnosed variants.

The hard, the soft, the red, white and blue, the cake and eat it, the Canada Dry and Norway plus, the deal or the no deal. But as it did so, the clock, as Michel Barnier, the European Union's chief negotiator, was now fond of repeating, was ticking.

Instead of the promise of frictionless trade the immediate prognosis seemed only to offer tradeless friction. As Project Fear revealed itself to be Project Reality. Not that they had not been warned.

For the Scots, whilst the prospect of being denied their status as European citizens against their will would, on the face of it, seem to provide a welcome boost to the nationalist cause, the reality was more nuanced.

The General Election in 2015, following their defeat in the independence referendum, had seen the Scottish National Party achieve an almost clean sweep. But then last year's post-Brexit rerun saw the Conservatives, the party of Brexit, double their share of Scotland's vote.

The Scots' appetite for Independence was still strong, and maybe, as the polls suggested, it was even now growing, but the party that offered the only realistic hope of ever achieving it was starting to look like it was losing a bit of its lustre.

It had been in Government for getting on for fifteen years now. It had become The Establishment that it once sought to overthrow. And, as such, to the young, and not only the young, it no longer had the radicalism or the energy of the insurgent. Its former leader would soon be the subject of complaints of serious sexual misconduct. He would be arrested and charged, and subsequently tried and acquitted, but not before the party would come close to tearing itself apart.

To Frank, and not only to Frank, it all looked like a bit of a mess. And not one that looked like it was going to get any better before it got a good deal worse.

# 13. The Shortbread Tin

Frank had always told anyone who was prepared to listen, and plenty more who were not, that he considered Ryanair to have done more to implement freedom of movement in the European Union than anyone else.

Without Ryanair, there would be no plumbers from Poznan in Portobello, for sure, and no Vets from Vilnius either. Not that Global Britain would soon be in any need of either.

Frank had a particular admiration for Michael O'Leary, Ryanair's founder and Chief Executive, for the unique way in which he had single-mindedly built his business on price, and price alone.

For how he couldn't care less if anybody liked him, and, in fact, consistently seemed to go out of his way to ensure that they did not. And for the effortless way in which he continually managed to annoy European Commissioners.

Anyway, he was not about to pay Brussels Airlines, the only other option open to him, the same as the price of a ticket to New York, for a biscuit and the convenience of arriving at Zaventem rather than Charleroi.

He had always found Ryanair to be punctual and reliable, just so long as you carefully followed their instructions to the letter. And did exactly what they told you to do, at exactly the time that they told you to do it.

Tomorrow morning, he would walk the five minutes from Harling Drive up Station Hill to catch the train to Glasgow Central. From there he would walk to Killermont Street and take the Express Bus to Edinburgh Airport, for which he had already booked his ticket online. He would be there in plenty of time to check in two hours before his flight.

He would pick up some underwear for Fiona, something that she liked him to do when travelling. And a Lego set, possibly an aeroplane, he thought, for Gabriel. And, of course, some shortbread and a tub of miniature Tunnock's Caramel Wafers, which, for some reason, seemed only ever to be available at Edinburgh airport.

He would land at Charleroi at six o'clock, take the bus into Brussels and get off at the stop on the corner of Chaussee de Waterloo and Avenue Lepoutre.

He would be back in the apartment on Rue Tenbosch before eight, all being well.

As he packed his holdall, Frank found that he was not only looking forward to being home, and being with Fiona but also, unusually, that he was looking forward to the journey itself. He folded his suit and his shirt, and he placed them in his holdall.

And then he went in search of a bag to carry those of the drawings that he had selected to take back home with him. The rest he would leave next door with Tom and Catherine for now. He was in no hurry to come to any decision about what to do with the rest of the contents of the house.

Nor for that matter, what to do with the house itself.

He opened the double wardrobe in Bill's bedroom. On the floor, at the front, besides three pairs of spiked golf shoes, was what he was looking for. A blue, leather, vintage Slazenger Golf kitbag with two long shoulder straps. The sort of thing Frank would have chosen for himself, he thought, had he ever found himself in need of a kitbag.

As he lifted it by one of the straps, the other caught on something beneath. He crouched down and released it from the door handle of a small grey metal box that was sitting unseen beneath it.

It was a safe, of the kind more usually found in hotel bedrooms, and so although Frank was a little puzzled at first to find it here in his father's wardrobe, he was not at all surprised to find that, when he entered the six digits of Bill's date of birth on its keypad, it opened.

Inside was a shortbread tin, a large shortbread tin, but nothing else. From the weight of it in his hand, Frank assumed at first that it was empty. But it was not.

He sat down on his father's bed. And once he had discarded the scorecards signed by Bill, Tom, Ian, and Doctor Livingstone, and others whose names he did not recognise, he began to count the banknotes.

There was the odd hundred, but most were fifties and twenties, so it took him a while, but when he had finished, he had counted out eight thousand pounds, or a little short of ten thousand euro. He took two hundred, that would cover the shopping, and save him the trouble of finding a cashpoint tomorrow. He put the rest back in the tin and then folded the tin carefully into the clothes in his holdall.

And so Sunday dawned, and all went according to Frank's plan.

He removed his shoes, his belt, his watch and his jacket, and placed his phone, his wallet, his cigarettes and his lighter, and his passport and his boarding card in the tray, just exactly as the animated instructions on the screen demanded.

But as his stockinged feet stepped through the metal detector, he felt the unfamiliar touch of authority on his shoulder. "Is this your bag, sir? And did you pack it yourself?" The words were spoken by a man maybe ten or fifteen years younger than Frank. He wore a cheap suit. He reminded Frank of someone, but, for the moment, he could not think exactly who.

The man seemed inexplicably pleased with himself, pleased to have something to do, and pleased to have someone, anyone, to tell that he was not from airport security, but HM Customs And Excise. The concealment, as he put it, of a large amount of cash in Frank's hand baggage was unusual, would Frank not agree? Though it was not, itself, necessarily an offence.

He would like to know nonetheless where the money had come from, why Frank was taking it to Belgium, and what he intended to do with it there. Frank told him about his father's death, and he offered his condolences, both personally and on behalf of HM Customs And Excise.

Frank told him that he believed it to be the proceeds of bets made between his father and his golfing friends over many years. He explained that he had discovered it only yesterday, a Saturday and that today being a Sunday, he had had no opportunity to deposit it in the bank before he had to return to work in Brussels.

The man poked about in Frank's holdall. He opened his shopping bags and examined Fiona's underwear, Gabriel's Lego, and the shortbread and Caramel Wafers without comment.

After what seemed to Frank to be an unnecessary length of time, he finally said: "In that case, I think I can let you be on your way, but perhaps in future, it would be better if you were to try and avoid any suspicion of money laundering".

"Money laundering" Frank repeated. "Yes, you'd be surprised how much of it goes on under such seemingly plausible excuses, a little here, a little there, it all adds up". Frank said nothing. "The maximum amount of currency that may be legally taken into, or out of, the European Union, by the way, is ten thousand Euro."

He seemed to spit the words 'European Union' but perhaps that was just Frank's imagination.

Were these people born passive-aggressive, he wondered, or was it something that they were trained in? Renaud, yes, that was it, he reminded him of Renaud. "Have a nice flight, sir."

If bags full of cash were such a concern then why didn't HM Customs And Excise spend more time poking about in the hand baggage of hedge fund managers coming back from Luxembourg or Zurich? Or football agents, for that matter.

His flight was called, and he boarded. He stowed his holdall in the rack. He took his extra legroom seat, and he fastened his seat belt.

He bought a ham and tomato sandwich, two miniatures of Famous Grouse, and a bottle of Highland Spring Water from the Slovakian steward.

Politely declining the offer of a lottery scratch card.

## 14. Strangers

It was the first time that Frank could ever remember Renaud addressing him directly without Frank having first asked him a question. "I was sorry to hear your news, my sincere condolences."

Hearing the word sincere on Renaud's lips was also a novelty. But, what is it they say? Everything stops for death. Even animosity, it seems."To you, and your family, and those of my department too, of course".

Or maybe not, 'and to your family' was an obvious provocation. Renaud's corduroy trousers today were mustard yellow. Frank almost thought that he preferred the red.

It was the first time that the two men had met for some months. After the summer vacation, there was something of a back to school, or rentree, as Renaud would have it, mood among the sixty or more people in the room. Most were familiar faces, but as well as the usual seasonal crop of fresh-faced interns, there were a couple of older faces.

He did not know them, but they had a familiar look about them.

The meeting had been in his agenda for some months. It had been billed as a kick-off for the strategy, narrative, and messaging development for the European Elections the following May.

As such, it was something that Frank's unit could have been expected to take an important, if not a leading role, in. As it always had done in the years before Frank's elevation. But today it appeared that Renaud was in charge, or even more in charge than usual.

It was he who sat to the Director's right, at the table placed in front of the theatre seating that accommodated Frank, his colleagues from various other units, and the interns.

Felix Eder, the Director, was a tall, thin-lipped, and rather pompous, Austrian. He had come from Finance and had only been in post since the spring. Nonetheless, the consensus already seemed to be that he had risen some way above his capabilities and that this was likely as far as he would be going. Not that getting as far as a Director was in any way a modest achievement.

He had no personal hinterland that anyone seemed to be aware of, and Frank thought that he would not be entirely surprised to discover that there were compromising photographs of him in existence somewhere.

And that, if there were, then Renaud most likely had access to them. Frank may even have shared such suspicions, but that was something else that he couldn't remember.

Eder addressed the room in a sombre mood, not, it must be said, that he was much of a comedian at the best of times. It was surely not a coincidence that his family name translated as ' he who dwells in a dark place'. Though that may not have been common knowledge in his Directorate, it was certainly unfortunate that that was the name that he was known by. Still, it was probably preferable to Felix, a name that to Frank brought to mind a brand of cat food.

It would not be, Eder said, an understatement to say that the events of the last two years in the United Kingdom had cast a long shadow on us and our vital work. But it was true also that it had focussed minds on the gravity of the situation that we now all faced together.

And on the vital importance of the success of the election campaign in overcoming the existential threat that we all now face, Frank waited for the word, together.

So far, so predictable, he wondered why none of them ever seemed to be able to bring themselves to say the word Brexit. The fear that it would only serve to encourage talk of such possible Anglo-Saxon derivations of the form as Frexit or Polexit?

Which if unlikely, were not entirely impossible either.

Or could they simply not bring themselves to face the fact that one of the Union's largest members was about to just fuck off? That Brexit had happened, or at least that it was happening. And on their watch.

But at least the Director had been clear, which was another welcome break with tradition. A room full of Eurocrats was being told by their boss that their jobs were on the line. As he, no doubt, had already been told by his boss, and his boss, no doubt, had already been told by his boss, and so on, as they say, ad infinitum.

Frank was hearing it with his own ears. They were not scared, but they were worried. And that also was a welcome break with tradition.

For a moment, Frank felt almost optimistic. And then Renaud rose to speak.

He had a high-pitched, rather whining, voice, not unlike a French-speaking David Beckham. He began in French, as he always did. But it was clear that the two men on his left were not following him. One had a word in Eder's ear, and Eder asked Renaud to continue in English.

It was not the first time, it was a regular occurrence, and, to be fair, not only when Renaud was addressing a meeting. In a room of Hungarians and Czechs and Poles and Latvians, not to mention Irish, Cypriots and Maltese, the common language was English, not French.

And yet still that remained a contentious issue for those older Francophones who remembered simpler, happier, times.

The war that they were about to engage in was nothing less than a war for our shared democratic values as Europeans, a war for democracy itself, Renaud said in what was pretty close to fluent, if heavily accented and rather irritable, English.

Renaud was not an engaging public speaker in any language. Words that on others' lips might have inspired and energised felt flat and sounded insincere.

It was a war that would be fought and won, he said, online.

Frank groaned, sufficiently audibly to raise a knowing smile and then a sly glance, from Izidora, a Croatian colleague, and a former lover. It had been a long time since they had spoken, but there was warmth in her smile.

To that end, two experts in online campaigning, senior experts, were there ever any other kind, Frank wondered, would be taking a key role in Renaud's team. Both had extensive experience working for Conservative Central Office in London.

More recently, they had worked on secondment to the Remain campaign. Where they had designed and implemented state-of-the-art online campaigning tools that placed social media platforms, and Facebook in particular, at the heart of communities of engaged voters.

Frank looked at the floor, wishing that it would open up and swallow him whole. But the fact that the campaign would be led by the Taliban and conducted largely, if not entirely, online was not any great surprise.

When you're a hammer, as the saying goes, everything looks like a nail.

But social media platforms, and Facebook in particular?

He could imagine this might make some sort of sense to Renaud, Renaud had no knowledge or experience of anything else, but Eder. And The Director-General?

What could they possibly be thinking?

Surely they had heard of Cambridge Analytica? Surely they were aware of the scale of the theft and abuse of personal data by 'social media platforms and Facebook in particular.'

Surely they knew that it had all been done in the course of political campaigning? For Brexit and Trump?

Surely they knew that it was all a scam? A scam that Facebook in the US had already been fined five billion dollars for its part in?

Surely Renaud, or his British experts at least, knew that even in the UK, they had been fined half a million pounds for the criminal offence, described with typically British understatement, of 'failing to safeguard people's information?

Surely they had heard of the Delete Facebook campaign that had even eventually forced an apology from Mark Zuckerberg, no less, for the first, and no doubt also the last, time in his life?

The scam was simple, as the best scams always are, and had been perpetrated in plain sight by posting bogus personality tests on Facebook. Fiona enjoyed them, despite Frank's suspicions.

On social media, if something is free, he had told her, then you may be sure that you are the product.

And yet here he was, listening to his colleagues if not yet embracing criminal behaviour themselves then planning to partner with convicted criminals.

The very same people who had, for the last two years, and for who knows how long before that, knowingly aided and abetted deliberate attempts to subvert the democracy that we were going to war to defend.

The arsonists were to be the firemen. The lunatics had taken over the asylum.

Izidora's eyes met his again, briefly, and then both looked away.

Renaud and his experts were now taking questions. Eder had left the room. A Swedish woman, whom Frank remembered from the discussion about what did, and what did not, constitute heteronormative imagery, was asking a question about Snapchat.

Frank felt the urgent need for nicotine. On the terrace, there was already a chill in the autumn afternoon air. It was going to be a long hard winter.

# 15. Not Before Time

It was an Anglo-Saxon problem.

Facebook's transgressions, for which, as Frank himself had acknowledged, they had apologised and claimed to have now fixed, had been in the US and the UK.

Trump and Brexit, neither had been good for Europe, but perhaps, in the long run, neither would turn out to be that bad for Europe either, not that we should ever say that.

There were plenty, after all, who had always wanted to be rid of the British."Not that you identify as British, these days though, I imagine." Eder raised his eyebrows at the word 'identify'.

It was Eder who had asked for their one-on-one. He wanted to explain his actions, he said, quickly adding, that had no need to, but that he wanted to. And, in any case, he did not like large meetings.

Frank was an underused asset, the DG had said so himself. Renaud's experts need not concern him, they were Renaud's responsibility.

And, strictly between themselves, there were still some unresolved issues around their online campaigning tools and the question of data privacy.

"What is it, you like to say? When you are a hammer?" Frank could not remember ever having said it to Eder, nor Renaud, for that matter, but at least it seemed to amuse him.

"Yes, of course, social media is a Faustian pact, but it is a necessary one. The politicians are on Facebook, all of them, all of the time, it's where their voters are. Are you going to tell them that they should not be?" His thin lips formed a small smile.

"Well, I wish you good luck with that, Frank." The smile broadened.

"Every politician is an expert in two things, one of them is defence, and the other?" He answered his question a beat before Frank could "is communication."

Frank had been expecting a telling off, perhaps even some sort of a warning.

"And they are our masters, Frank, please do not forget that." But none seemed to be coming.

Eder was candid, but he was complimentary, almost friendly.

Frank need not concern himself with the detail of the channels, there were plenty of people who would look after all that.

No, what he, and the DG, wanted and expected of Frank was that he bring his historian's brain to writing the narrative on which the campaign would be based. To 'drawing the big picture as he put it.

The strategy would be determined by those above them. And the messaging by Renaud's people, with whom he now expected Frank to put away his differences, to be more cooperative, and less confrontational. He would have the same conversation with Renaud, he said, and he would tell him that he expected the same.

But the meat in the sandwich, as he put it, would be Frank's responsibility. And he would personally make sure that Frank had access to all the resources that he needed.

Cara, Eder's assistant, appeared and cleared away the coffee cups. The meeting was over. Frank could already see Renaud waiting outside for his turn. And he took a childish pleasure in realising that he knew something that Renaud did not, and therefore being, if only for a moment or two, ahead of the game.

He thanked Eder for his time. The elevator doors closed behind him. He checked his eyes in the mirror, now more out of habit than anything else. A pang of guilt, familiar from his Father's funeral, hit him. He had known nothing about Eder, and yet, he had judged him, and harshly. He had been wrong. The Director's apparent pomposity was simply a dislike of large groups of people, a shyness. And he was far from humourless. He had been almost paternal, sympathetic certainly, and Frank was surprised to find himself now almost warming to him.

He wondered if he played golf.

The joke about the compromising photographs had been unnecessary, foolish and childish. It had been beneath him, and he regretted it.

He was learning, if not before time.

On the terrace, he lit a cigarette. And he decided there and then that he would focus his energies on what he had been asked to do. And through a winter that passed quickly, and turned out to be surprisingly mild, that is what he did.

Drafting narratives in the knowledge that they could also be maps, practical and instructive. Representations of what democracy should look like, its specifications, and its tolerances.

Taking on his father's work.

He found himself becoming more creative and more communicative. And he found that being in Fiona's company helped him with that.

She was never far from his side in those months, and Bill was never far from his thoughts, as he now began to find beauty in meaning and meaning in beauty.

And the formidable superpower that is the two together.

# 16. The Last Hill

History teaches us that it is necessary only for good men to do nothing for bad men to prevail.

Frank could not now recall who it was who had said it, or where he had read it but it sounded like a good place to start.

As, not before time, he began to awake from the state of suspended animation that had enabled him to survive his childhood and navigate adulthood thus far. That it was Fiona's love that had begun the gradual process of his defrosting was true.

But it had been Bill's unexpected death that had accelerated it. In the gaining of understanding, in the finding of appreciation, in the reevaluation, not just of his father's life, but of his own, Frank found a higher gear.

There was history not only in the past, but in the present also, and in the future.

Maybe the answer was to take what we could find that represented what was common to us from the past and the present and take it with us to map our future.

There have always been alternatives to democracy and there still are, there are plenty of places where monarchy and theocracy still work.

But once democracy has been chosen, or has emerged, and is established, the most common threat to it comes not from Kings or Mullahs, but autocrats.

From bad men and from good men who do nothing.

In the language of Frank's employers, trips out of the office, trips out into the real world to conferences, or even to their own Liaison Offices in the member states, were known as Missions, the theocratic overtones of the word being, he presumed, entirely accidental.

They were rare, involving so much administration and so many levels of approval, so much signing, and so much countersigning, as to be effectively discouraged.

Those few colleagues who lived and worked in the real world most often came to Brussels instead. And so it was on their Missions that these Poles, Romanians, Czechs, Slovakians, and Slovenians began to help Frank to develop his thinking.

He spent long hours with them, in Chez Martine or Au Laboureur, in discussion of their various pasts and presents. Sharing in their knowledge and their experience of bad men and of good men who did nothing.

And with them, he discovered a sense of purpose, a mission of his own, a Mission, in fact, worthy of the name, and of its capital M.

He felt the rhythm of history repeating itself. And slowly he began to feel, as much as to think, what it was that represented what was common to us from the past and the present, and how it might come to map the future.

And so the drawing of the big picture began to take shape. The representation of what democracy could look like, its specifications, and its tolerances. The meat in Eder's sandwich. It did not come easily, and it did not come quickly.

Its formulation was not Frank's, or at least it was not Frank's alone. It was not something that he would ever claim credit for, for, in reality, it was his father's work, and Fiona's also.

And once copied and circulated it would prove at first to be a useful guide to democracy's machinists and fitters in Brussels, and then to those responsible for its upkeep and maintenance in Calais and Dusseldorf and Athens and Naples. 'On social media platforms, and Facebook in particular' or for that matter in ink on paper.

Autocrats do not start as autocrats, or at least, they do not declare themselves to be so. They are populists. Men, for they are inevitably men, of the people. They are skilled at articulating popular current concerns, or grievances, for which they blame others; migrants, Muslims, Jews, homosexuals, judges, journalists, the educated, and the elite.

It doesn't matter, so long as those to blame are others, unlike us. The autocrat's goal is division, and through it, power.

But what then are democrats? They also seek power, but they seek it, not by apportioning blame to others for the present, but rather by asking us to share responsibility for the future. And what could be more responsible than the act of voting?

How could that responsibility be better shared than by each of us all having one, and only one, vote? No matter our religion, our job, our education, our wealth, or whom we choose to share a bed with.

Eder was nodding. "If we are saying that the difference between a democrat and a populist is that the democrat takes responsibility for the future, while the populist blames others for the present, then yes, that is true."

Frank lent forward in his seat and he carried on "Which means that in a democracy the power of the people will always triumph over the people in power?"

"No, that's never going to fly." In the past, Frank had often wondered why whenever they spoke of the rejection, or rather the non-validation, of an idea, the hierarchy invariably used the metaphor of flight.

That Eder considered the second part, the more interesting part, in Frank's mind, of the narrative, simply not airworthy was expected, but it was significant.

"The first bit, yes, I will be glad to take that upstairs for validation, and I can see nothing in it that the DG, and even the Secretary-General, would not be happy with."

A representation of democracy was all well and good, but there was no need to get into its precise specifications, far less its tolerances. That was dangerous territory, and best left to others.

"The politicians, our masters, Frank, they are the people in power, and you make it sound as if you are trying to frighten them." He was right, of course, and Frank knew it.

"And to be honest with you, perhaps more honest than I should be, right now they are quite frightened enough as it is."

Eder smiled, and his assistant, Cara, appeared, were they telepathic? Frank wondered, or was there a hidden button somewhere that Eder pressed when he wished to end a meeting?

"Good work, Frank," he said, quietly, almost as if to himself, as Frank left the room. Frank heard his words, of course, as he was meant to, and he smiled with a degree of entirely justified selfsatisfaction as he examined his eyes in the mirror of the elevator.

But perhaps now that was an affectation that he could leave behind him. The whole undead thing, it was another thing that was unnecessary, something else that now seemed foolish and childish and beneath him.

He descended to take a valedictory cigarette on the terrace, before heading home to dinner with Fiona, and he remembered the truth of Peter Galbraith's wisdom on the subject of excelling in examinations.

And, in his mind, he thanked him for it. For what had he just done but persuade the examiner to believe that he knew a good deal more than he did, or ever would.

"Hello, Frank" The unseen voice was unmistakable, and pleasantly so.

It belonged to Izidora, who now appeared without warning, and without any obvious indication of where she had come from. Perhaps he had a hidden button in his coat that he was unaware of and had pressed by accident as he did sometimes with his phone. Or perhaps she did.

She was on her way home, dressed in a green zipped and quilted coat, of the kind that he liked to describe as a sleeping bag, and a white wooden scarf. The colour of her coat perfectly matched her eyes.

She was as beautiful as ever, he thought, maybe even a little more so than he remembered. She wore her hair long now, and she seemed softer somehow, less conservative in her dress for sure.

He felt a need to talk to her.

"You're smiling," she said, "it suits you." He held the door open, and she followed him out onto the terrace. She did not seem to be in any hurry to go home. They sat down together on the edge of an elevated, but apart from discarded cigarette buts, entirely barren, flowerbed.

He lit a cigarette and she took one from his pack. "Please," she said. "You didn't use to smoke," he said. "And you didn't use to smile." Frank laughed. She took his arm and leant her head against his for a moment. "I heard about your father," she said. Frank said nothing, but he did not feel at all uncomfortable.

She told him that she was happy to hear that he had at last decided to be as clever as she knew he was, as everyone knew he was. She told him that people were talking about him, and that good things were being said about him.

She proposed that they meet for a coffee, soon, and she said that she was not just saying that, but that she meant it.

Or for a drink after work, maybe, if that was what he would prefer. Frank said that he would like to do that and that he meant it also. They walked down the stairs together, she to the car park, and he out into the night.

He crossed Rue Belliard, into Parc Leopold, and past The House Of European History. An institution which he had long argued would be much better named The House Of European Histories.

And it struck him again that, although it had never been meant as a joke, that was perhaps another unnecessarily provocation that was probably also now better left behind.

Or maybe not, it was true, after all. It was the fact that there was a plurality of European Histories that had got them as far as an almost, nearly, maybe, validated, election narrative. Besides, it would be premature, he thought, to completely erase all traces of the Frank of former years.

But then again, what is it that they say? What is not premature, often turns out to be too late. He laughed to himself. As clever as she knew he was, yes, he liked that.

On the far side of the park, he caught the Number 60 Bus to Place Brugmann.

Fiona was waiting for him at a table on the terrace at Plasch. She was drinking a glass of champagne and smoking a cigarette. The very picture of beauty and elegance.

It was almost November, and although there was the first smell of winter in the air, it was still a pleasantly mild evening. Frank was happy to see her and excited to be able to share his news. He sat down, and she leaned across the table to kiss him.

There was an unfamiliar smell on him, she thought, the smell of a woman. And he was late. The maitre d' appeared."Champagne, sir, and one more for madame, or perhaps you would prefer just to finish the rest of the bottle?"

The rest of the bottle? How much had she already drunk? He wasn't that late. He nodded his agreement. It was a Thursday and they did have something to celebrate.

"And a bottle of petillante, and a cheeseburger, a point, for me, and...?" Fiona finished her glass and lit another cigarette. "I'm not hungry, Frank," she said. "I had lunch."

The Maitre d' returned with an ice bucket and rather less than half a bottle of champagne. He refilled Fiona's glass and poured one for Frank.

The two men looked at each other, and without a word being spoken, they apprised the delicacy of the situation, and how it would best be resolved.

"You should eat something," Frank said. The Maitre d' concurred. "An omelette crevette, perhaps, madame?"

It was not turning out to be the evening that Frank had expected, or had wanted. But then again, when had Fiona ever been, or done, what he expected?

That was part of the thrill of it, or it had been anyway. It was not as if she was getting any worse, it was just perhaps that he was getting a bit better. She toyed with her omelette and ate Frank's frites. "I don't want to talk about your work," she said.

She did not want a dessert or a coffee. And the maitre d' was a wise enough man not to offer a digestif on the house this evening.

Frank paid, and they walked down Avenue Lepoutre together. Fiona leant into him and took his arm. More for support tonight than in affection.

He helped her into the apartment. She took off her coat and she disappeared into the bathroom. Frank poured a whisky, kicked off his shoes, and lay down on the sofa.

He turned on the TV and he watched English people blaming each other for Brexit on Question Time on the BBC. It was a show that he had once enjoyed, but it was a long time now since he ever made a point of watching it. Tonight he found it ill-tempered, angry even. Like so much of Britain now, or so much of England, anyway.

The audience's questions, such as they were, seemed trite. There was little thought in the panellists' answers and certainly no respect among them. The debate, or the argument, for it was nothing more than that, was certainly a long way from his conversation with Eder this evening.

Why was it, he wondered, not for the first time, that English politics was so wary of the big picture, so big on blame and so lacking in responsibility? The irresponsibility, the disregard for the consequences of their actions, now more and more often dressed up in glorious tales of Empire. Fiona had never once even come close to mentioning the British when she spoke of India, which she often did, but as Frank had read only the other day, in an article on Brexit by an Indian journalist, even once the British have decided to leave, they take a very long time going about it.

He was finding Question Time grating on his ears now. These days he found he had less and less interest in British politics. As seen from Brussels it just looked more and more irrelevant. He turned off the TV.

He brushed his teeth, undressed, and went to bed, where, sure enough, he found Fiona, fast asleep, under the covers, fully clothed.

She had managed to remove her boots, but not her makeup. Her eyes were smudged, she had been crying. Her phone lay on the pillow, its illuminated screen open on her Facebook page. He closed it and plugged it into the charger on her side of the bed.

He closed his eyes, and, in the moment before sleep came, he reflected on the events of what had been a busy, but in the end, a mixed sort of a day.

And he reflected too on his mixed sort of a life these last few months. For the first time in his life, he felt, not just engaged, but energised by his work.

Was it that that was now disengaging him from Fiona? And she from him? Or was there more to it than that?

His last conscious thought was of Izidora. There had been a sadness in her eyes. There had always been a trace of it there, but something seemed to be on her mind.

As sleep came he found himself puzzling as to why she had married Renaud's friend Philippe. He recalled the wedding, and he remembered having thought then that she did look much like a woman who was having the happiest day of her life.

Renaud was the best man, and his speech, in French, of course, had been mostly about his adventures with the groom, he barely mentioned the bride. But Frank had not been to many weddings, and had been told by those who had that that was the tradition.

He remembered talking with Izidora's parents, he had been on his own, having not yet met the Dutch girl.

He remembered her mother's ill-disguised irritation at the best man's inattention to the non-French speakers in the room, who were, after all, in the majority.

Yes, he would see Izidora for a drink, or lunch, or dinner maybe. It had been a long time since they had spoken. And twelve years since they had last slept together.

# 17. Isolation

It was now already three years, and even her husband had barely lasted four.

The anchor of Fiona's longing was coming loose. Losing its purchase as the tides turned. It would be some time yet before it finally worked itself free, and the process would not be without pain or consequences. There would be many good days still to come, and when they did then the bad ones somehow seemed of less importance.

She took more interest in and spent more time with, her gurus now.

While Frank allowed himself a moment's reflected, if not glory, for that was not his style, then satisfaction at least.

The Election Campaign had worked. It had worked better, in fact, than any previous campaign. It had increased turnout by double-digit percentages among some age groups in some member states. For the first time in history, more than half of Europe's voters had made the effort to vote.

The hierarchy began to talk more, and louder, about the Parliament's democratic legitimacy. It had a newfound confidence, a swagger, almost. Even persuading itself, if not entirely convincing others, that Ursula von der Leyen, a woman whom not even Frank had ever heard of six weeks ago, had at least, in a strictly technical sense, been democratically elected as President of The European Commission.

He began to find himself invited to take part in Missions. He went to Budapest and Ljubljana, Rome and Madrid, and Berlin.

He went to Zagreb with Izidora, and they had dinner with her mother. And he extended a trip to Copenhagen to take in a weekend at Legoland with Fiona and Gabriel.

But it was an unintended consequence, and an unfortunate irony, that as both Frank and Renaud began to build upon their successful collaboration or at least their successful cessation of hostilities, they began to be trusted to take on more work in-house.

And so they found themselves in less need of the services of the contractors than they once had.

Fiona now had less work than she had been used to. And being employed freelance, having less work meant having less money.

To make matters worse, Geert was now starting to become difficult about maintenance, Lies was expecting their daughter in the new year.

Frank told her, on more than one occasion, that he would not see them starve, and he meant it. But then again, he had no way of knowing what was coming.

And he had no way of stopping it either, no one had.

He was in the business lounge at Zaventem, waiting to board a flight to Rome, when he heard his name called. He was travelling on his British Passport which he was now asked to show.

Britain was no longer a Member of the EU, but Frank's employers did not seem to have noticed. Or at least, if they had, at least they were saying nothing about it, for now. That however did not seem to be the problem this morning.

Had he visited China at any time in the last thirty days? Or had he been in close contact with anyone who had, or might have?

He had read about SARS COVID-19, but he was not alone in being completely unprepared for the speed at which COVID-19, as it quickly became known, before it became just COVID, and then, finally and simply, the pandemic, was about to sweep the world.

Nor for the existential questions that it would ask of him, and Fiona, and of their relationship, Nor the countless ways in which it would change not only his life but life itself.

Frank did not know Rome well, but it had always been somewhere that he had enjoyed visiting. To any historian, every footstep in the city was like a field trip.

He liked the fact that every Roman, from shop assistants to anarchists, took care in their dress, and took pride, not only in their appearance but in the nobility of being Roman.

He liked the noise, and the energy, and the food, of course, and the strict timetable around its consumption that required you to eat Gnocchi on a Thursday and Ravioli on a Friday, and not the other way round. And never to order a Cappuccino after eleven o'clock.

He liked Fabrizio, his bald, bespectacled, Calabrian colleague, who ran the Liaison Office. He had been one of Frank's more enthusiastic, and also most helpful, collaborators last year.

Fabrizio had instinctively understood what was needed and had brought not only a knowledge and an experience of Italian history, but an understanding of US politics that had turned out to be surprisingly helpful as they grappled with the idea of what was, and what was not European.

He had taken his Masters in Politics at UCLA and perfected his spoken English, which was liberally punctuated with the words 'motherfucker' and 'dude' while working in a record store in Westwood. He was both an election nerd and a fan of classic rock. His grandfather was a farmer.

He liked whisky, and the occasional spliff, and Scotland, and Scots. He respected the fact that the Romans had, as he put it, taken one look at the Scots and decided that it would be better just to leave them be and build a wall. He respected that, and it amused him.

Frank liked the fact that their best, and most productive discussions in Brussels had always taken place in Chez Martine. It was obvious that Fabrizio had also felt at home there.

He was happy to see Frank again but sorry about 'all this bullshit' Not everyone was yet wearing face masks or rubbing their hands with sanitising gel. It was not as bad as in the North, apparently, but it did look like it was only going to get worse.

They ate dinner at Melo, a Sicilian restaurant, around the corner from the office, where it was clear from the moment that they entered that Fabrizio was an habituato.

It was packed, unusually so, according to Fabrizio. Those without reservations were being politely turned away. It was a Tuesday night in February, and yet, it felt like Christmas or New Year. It was, Fabrizio and the proprietor agreed, all a little strange.

There was something of an end of days feeling about it all.

Fabrizio ordered the Farsu Magru, square stuffed veal slices topped with bacon, it was the house speciality, he explained, and you certainly would not find better this side of Palermo. He insisted that Frank have the same, which he did.

They shared a bottle of Montepulciano. But it was clear that Fabrizio was not himself, he had seemed fine this afternoon, but now something was troubling him.

His mother had been admitted to hospital earlier this evening, she was eighty-two and it was not the first time. But it was the first time that he had been told that neither he nor his brother would be allowed to visit her. Fabrizio was worried, what if it was COVID-19?

The Italian Government had announced that travel into and out of the most affected regions was to be prohibited from midnight tomorrow.

He was sorry to have to say so but he thought that it would be better if Frank were to return to Brussels tomorrow rather than on Friday, as planned.

He had already changed Frank's ticket. He was now booked on the Alitalia flight from Fumicino at ten o'clock tomorrow morning. It looked more than likely that the border would soon be closed. However much the

Commission would try to resist that.

Schengen would unravel, he predicted, and with it the freedom of movement granted by the treaty of, where else but Rome? And without freedom of movement, what good was the European Union to anyone?

"But you are a historian, Frank, you know that Empires never last."

We would all soon enough be back to the days of passports and border controls.

There was already some talk of vaccines, that had been how viruses had been defeated, or at least, managed, in the past. The British said that they were already working on one, and the Chinese too, and the Russians.

Fabrizio drank his wine, and he wondered aloud if maybe when they came, the vaccines would not have something to do with some new kind of passport. The British would like that, they liked passports, depending on what colour they were, of course.

A passport granted, not on your nationality, but according to your health. The world would be divided into the clean and the unclean.

And the undead, Frank thought but kept the thought to himself.

It was an interesting thesis, but one that, even for Frank, was just too depressing for this evening. He put it down to Fabrizio's preoccupation with his mother's health and the wine.

"And how long did it take to stitch my country back together, after our Empire fell?"

Frank let him go on, though he wasn't listening now. "Garibaldi," he said, and for a moment Frank thought that he meant the biscuit.

"Queen Victoria" he was rambling "Vladimir Putin, Ursula von der Leyen". He laughed. For the first time today. And Frank thought that he maybe sort of got what he meant now.

They did not take dessert, coffee, or a digestif, but as they walked back to Frank's hotel, Fabrizio seemed to sober up a bit, or at least to lighten up.

He remembered that there was a Scottish bar a couple of blocks further on. He would buy Frank a whisky there, it was the least that he could do, he said. And it was the least that he could do, Frank thought, to be enthusiastic about his host's late change of plan.

The Nags Head was a rugby bar with an admittedly impressive selection of Irish and English beers on tap. It served Traditional Scottish Stovies and something called a Pizza Wallace. But it still fell some way short of being 'Assapora Il Gusto Autentico Della Scozia' as the sign above the door claimed.

At least not if you were Scottish yourself, anyway.

The list of malts was short, and a bit of a disappointment. The bar was loud, a DJ was playing, and its clientele was young, very young. All Frank wanted to do was to go to bed.

Fabrizio eventually emerged from the scrum at the bar with two large Isle Of Jura 10-Year-Olds and a bottle of still water.

They took them outside to the relative quiet of the street, and they toasted each other's good health, which they both agreed, seemed especially appropriate this evening.

Fabrizio's cloud descended again: "Those motherfuckers will make trouble out of this." But Frank had now been distracted by a group of Italian girls Instagramming one another by the blue neon horse's head that was the pub sign.

They were young, students most likely, but one of them reminded him of Fiona. She had the same hair, tied up in the same style, and the same perfect skin. She wore a black leather skirt and a denim jacket.

He suddenly missed her and he wondered where she was now, and what she was doing. He checked his phone, but there were no messages.

"And it won't just be here in Italy either, Frank." The sound of his name jolted him out of his reverie and back to the here and now.

He realised that Fabrizio was talking about the virus. "Yeah, motherfuckers" he said, though he was not entirely sure which motherfuckers, he, or Fabrizio, for that matter, were talking about.

The populist motherfuckers? Or the Facebook motherfuckers?

The next morning Frank woke five minutes before his alarm. This often seemed to happen when he was travelling for some reason, but never at home.

There were two voice messages. Fiona said that she was missing him and that she wanted him to come home. She had read, on Facebook, of course, that people were dying in Italy. And that COVID 19 was some kind of Chinese biological weapon.

He called her back but there was no reply. She would be taking Gabriel to school. He told her that he was on his way back to Brussels now, that she was not to worry, and that he loved her.

The second was a broken, but unfamiliar, voice, and Frank struggled for a moment to place it, before the caller identified himself as Ian, the brother of his father's neighbour, Tom.

Tom had been taken short of breath on Sunday afternoon, he said. He had been taken into Ayr Infirmary on Monday morning and the doctors had hooked him up to a ventilator. He had died last night. And neither he nor Catherine had been allowed to see him.

Maybe Bill had been lucky to go when he did, after all, he said. And he told Frank to take care of himself.

Frank showered and packed. He checked out and took a cappuccino and a quick selection of colazione from the buffet in the hotel lobby and he waited for his taxi. The concierge handed him a face mask as he left.

He had expected the airport to be busy, but it was quiet, eerily so. He shopped for underwear and lego, cigarettes, a Panettoni, and a good bottle of Montepulciano.

He browsed the Whiskies, and there, among the island single malts, he found what he had been looking for, without really being aware that he was looking for anything at all.

A Talisker Twenty-Five Year Old, in a gift pack, appropriately, with two glasses. Tonight, they would drink to Tom's life and Bill's with this. They would remember the wake, and the night in Tom and Catherine's parlour, could it only be, not even two years ago?

And he and Fiona would once more reaffirm their love for one another. They would be ok, wouldn't they?

He walked to the gate. He passed through security. It would be a long time before he, or anyone else for that matter, would do either, or anything else so seemingly routine, again.

By then, Alitalia, and much else besides, would be gone for good.

# 18. Confinement

It would be a while before 'le lockdown' would become assimilated into the French Language.

For now, it was still 'le confinement.'

And it would be Dutch, not often considered even by its native speakers to be the language of love, that would provide the most endearing, if not the most enduring, expression of the pandemic, at least in Belgium.

The word knuffel was already familiar to Frank from the Laland Scots dialect that he had spoken as a child. In the schoolyard, at least, though not in the classroom, where to do so would only earn you a skelp, or a smack, on the head.

As snuffle was akin to a cold, so knuffel was akin to a cuddle.

Belgians, being practical and considerate people, were early to realise that there was no form of social distancing, however loosely enforced, that would ever be good for anyone's mental health. And so the concept of knuffelvriend, or cuddle friend, became established in Belgian Law.

The word itself was not new. Like the French nounours, a knuffelvriend is simply a teddy bear. Strictly speaking, it does not even have to resemble an actual bear. So long as it is a stuffed soft toy, it may, and often does, take any real, or imagined, animate form.

The concept of being someone's teddy bear was not new either. The Elvis Presley hit came to Frank's mind.

And he wondered if Colonel Tom Parker, Elvis's mysterious manager, had also been familiar with knuffelvrienden, he being a Dutchman by birth.

And what, The Colonel, as a man who lived his entire adult life confined to the US as an illegal immigrant, might have made of the rest of the world similarly confined to wherever they happened to now find themselves, with only their teddy bears for friends.

That Frank would find more time, and more cause, to consider such thoughts in the weeks and months to come, would stand him in good stead. For in such seeming randomness he would be happy to find things to hold onto in the dark days ahead.

The exact rules were complicated, they were Belgian, after all, but essentially, anyone living alone during le confinement was entitled to two nominated knuffelvrienden. They were not, as Fiona was not slow to point out, the same as sexbuddies. And you were also permitted to regularly change them on certain nominated days.

Gabriel, at least, was well up on the Dutch of it all, and, aside from some welcome levity, he was also able to take some reassurance from the fact that Frank would continue to be around now that Gabriel was no longer at school, and now that his mother and Frank were both working at home. After Frank's return from Rome, events unfolded quickly. As Fabrizio had predicted, Italy closed its schools, its shops, its bars, its restaurants and its borders that week. Spain followed, and then France and the Netherlands, and then, inevitably Belgium.

By now Belgium was reporting the third-highest number of COVID-19 deaths per head of population anywhere in the world. The mood in Brussels was sombre, even among Frank and Fiona's laissez-faire friendship group.

It was a Friday, Frank went into work early and had breakfast with Izidora. She was going back to Croatia with her daughter, Ana, while they could still travel. Schools and shops were closed but there was no lockdown in Zagreb, and things didn't sound quite so bad there yet, she said.

Frank walked her down to the garage and they said their farewells. And they kissed, hesitantly at first, unsure of whether or not they should, as former lovers often are.

Izidora began to cry. "Take good care of yourself, Frank," she said. "Please, for me." Frank did not know what to think, or what he felt. But he knew that he felt something.

He took the Metro to De Brouckere. And he met Fiona outside Delhaize. She was wearing a mask. They joined the queue.

And then they spent much of the rest of the day pushing Fiona's caddy back and forth between there and her apartment. Stocking her cupboards with pasta, tinned tomatoes, cheese, milk, and water, biscuits, and toilet rolls, for some reason, and wine and beer.

It was not just the toilet rolls, Frank really could not understand why any of this needed to be done at all. Shops were to remain open. And the government had asked people not to panic buy.

But it made her happy, it seemed to fulfil some need in her, and so despite Frank's, as it was to turn out, well-founded, suspicion that it was all, in some way, inspired by something that she had seen on Facebook, he did it willingly, or at least without comment or complaint.

They ate oysters and tuna together at The Noordzee just as they had done on their first date. And then, taking advantage of Gabriel's last afternoon at school, they made love in the kitchen.

That evening, they went to Chez Martine together, and they laughed together, and they spoke Dutch and French and English and Arabic with their accountant friend, and the academic, and the actor, and the builder, and the courier, and the graphic designers, and the IT man, and his musician friends, and the writer, and the nurse, and the secretary.

Tonight, everyone was here. All of them knowing, but none of them saying, that there was not one of them who knew when, or even if, they would ever all get to see each other again.

Selfies were taken and posted to Facebook, Instas were Grammed, whisky was drunk, and Auld Lang Syne was sung, As it was at New Year, when the French, at least, preferred to celebrate the 'fin d'annee' just gone, rather than the new one just arrived. Something that until now, Frank had thought odd, but that tonight suddenly seemed entirely logical.

It was gone three o'clock by the time that he finally managed to persuade Fiona to call it a night. She was drunk, they were both drunk, whisky drunk again. She took his arm and she leant into him. And tonight they helped each other home, stopping along the way to kiss and to knuffel.

Before Fiona collapsed on the bed, finally exhausted by all of the many efforts of her day. Frank undressed her and put her to bed. He undressed. And he lay down beside her. He caressed the perfect skin of her perfect body, and he saw again her beauty.

And he held her tightly in his arms, and he felt again her meaning. And he closed his eyes. He loved her. And he tried, with all the strength left in his drunken mind to find meaning in her beauty, and beauty in her meaning. They would be ok, wouldn't they?

Frank was awake, but still in bed when Geert arrived with Gabriel. There was a freshly made cup of coffee beside the bed, he sipped it.

He felt surprisingly clear-headed, but he did need a cigarette.

He got up, and pulled on his trousers, his shirt and a jumper. He went out onto the terrace. It was a clear day. There was even a little warmth in the spring sunshine.

There was not a cloud to be seen in the sky, and there was not a sound to be heard from the city. So this is how it will be, he thought, peaceful.

Of course, if nothing else, at least it will be peaceful.

And then he heard Fiona shouting, and then Gabriel crying, and then Geert, at least he assumed it was Geert, slamming the apartment door as he left.

He put out his cigarette in the oyster shell, and he took his coffee with him into the kitchen.

Gabriel met him heading in the opposite direction towards his room.

He quickly dried his tears, not wishing to appear unmanly.

Frank crouched down to his height. Gabriel came into his arms and hugged him tightly, almost spilling his coffee. It was the first time that they had seen each other since Frank's trip to Rome, three weeks ago, and Frank had missed him. As much, it seemed, as Gabriel had missed Frank. "I can stay here with you and mum, can't I," he said. "in the lockdown." Frank looked up at Fiona and she nodded. "Of course you can," he said. "Of course you can." And so reassured, Gabriel disappeared into his room and closed the door. Pausing only to throw a broad I told you so grin to his mother over his shoulder.

Frank shrugged and he laughed. "The apple does not fall far from the tree," he said."I'm sorry to wake you with that" Fiona kissed him, slowly and tenderly. More slowly, and more tenderly than yesterday, more slowly and more tenderly than for some time.

Perhaps, he thought, this could maybe turn out to be just what the two of them needed."I was already awake, and enjoying my coffee, thank you for that, by the way, and a cigarette. I was just thinking how quiet and peaceful lockdown was turning out to be, when... "

Fiona refilled Frank's coffee and she lit a cigarette. And then she followed him, first back to the terrace where they enjoyed a moment in the sun in the silence together. And then back to bed, where she put on the underwear that Frank had only seen so far in the shop in Fumicino Airport, and they spent the rest of the morning making love.

# 19. The Man

Spring turned to summer, slowly and, apart from Fiona's simmering conflict with Geert, for the most part, peacefully.

During this first confinement, the required social distancing was achieved by the creation of bubbles of a limited number of people who were permitted to visit one another's homes.

The nuclear family, of course, was one such bubble, but there were many others and they were of many different sizes, shapes and forms. And it was to Belgium's credit, it being a socially liberal place, that the rules were usually open to fairy generous interpretation, and only lightly enforced.

Geert, being Dutch, and rather less socially liberal than Fiona, or indeed Frank, was firmly against Gabriel's inclusion in Fiona and Frank's bubble from the outset.

His son, he argued, belonged with him and Lies, and their newborn daughter, in safe, suburban, Vilvoorde. Now that Gabriel was not attending school, he did not need to be with Fiona in Brussels, a likely, though not as it turned out to be in fact, a hotspot of the contagion.

In practice, there was nothing that Geert could do about it, and he knew that, but it was another way to increase the pressure on Fiona, and he knew that too.

The weather was kind, and, in those first weeks, Frank's first prognosis turned out to be entirely accurate. Brussels was a calmer, quieter place, Ste. Catherine especially so.

There were no tourists for one thing, and no aeroplanes, and very little traffic. In those early days, it soon became fashionable to talk of the pandemic as some sort of a pause, or a reset.

Even as a necessary one, a chance, perhaps the final chance, some said, for the World to confront the errors of its ways, and to choose a different path, a calmer, quieter, more thoughtful and less consumerist one maybe. Yes, perhaps this was what they needed. Like everyone else, Frank soon grew accustomed to the slow-moving queues outside Delhaize and Charlie, the local boulangerie, to keeping his distance from others, and even, eventually, to the curfew that required everyone to remain at home between 10:00 pm and 06:00 am.

To the endless hand sanitising, and to the face masks, which, as if they were not disorientating enough as it was, he was not alone in finding had the irritating habit of somehow slipping over your eyes, as well as your mouth and nose.

There was still some debate then about the efficacy of face masks. Some epidemiologists, the new soothsayers of the time, believed that the virus lived on surfaces, and that face masks were a distraction from regular, thorough, hand-washing, the wearing of gloves, and the spraying of everything with sanitising gel.

Frank didn't know, though surely it was significant that the doorman at the hotel in Rome had given him a face mask and not a pair of gloves. And that in those Asian countries with experience of a SARS pandemic, most people had continued to wear face-masks from that day to this.

But Fiona did know. And looking back on it, perhaps it was this first difference of opinion, about face masks, and about what they signified, as much as what they did, or did not do to offer protection against the virus, that was to form the first small fissure that would eventually widen into the gulf that would first come first to separate them, and then worse.

For just as Geert was powerless to enforce his views about Gabriel's bubble, so Frank was unable to prevent Facebook from becoming Fiona's primary, and very soon her only, source of information on all things in any way virus related. As pretty much everything in life had now become.

She showed Frank the certificate that she had obtained from her doctor exempting her from wearing a mask on medical grounds. She was asthmatic, she had told the doctor, no doubt with a smile. Not even attempting to hide the lie from Frank, she laughed, and she lit a cigarette. "Wake up, Frank," she said.

Even then, that first time, the phrase sounded patronising, and not a little threatening.

That her many gurus had always been Californian was not a coincidence. Though the fact that she drank and she smoked, and that she heartily, it could even properly be said, lustily, enjoyed eating the many, and varied, parts of animals that only Belgian cuisine could offer, made her an unlikely devotee of any commonly accepted definition of wellness.

Wellness was not something that Frank had ever been exposed to before he met Fiona. It was unknown in the Scotland of his youth and in the Universities that he had attended. And it was not something that they had ever spoken about before now.

He struggled to relate any of it to the Fiona that he knew, or at least to the Fiona that he thought he knew. And he didn't like the sound of its assumed moral superiority.

How could you, and you alone, be expected to be entirely responsible for your health, irrespective of the circumstances of your birth, your wealth, or your life chances?

Had his grandfather died of a stroke at the age of fifty-six because he had never seen an avocado, far less eaten one? It was nonsense, nobody deserved to be ill.

But with a little effort, and a good deal of thought, he found that he could at least begin to understand where the idea had come from.

And to appreciate why it made perfect sense to someone living in a city like Seattle, say. Someone who never missed her hot yoga class, who drank herbal tea and carrot juice, who didn't smoke and drank alcohol only rarely and socially, and who only ever shopped at the local whole food store. Someone like Fiona's mother, for example.

Not that he was any stranger to the Farm Cooperative on Chaussee de Waterloo, where he could be found recycling his own local source glass mineral water bottles and stocking up on bio beer and wine. But that was about the environment, wasn't it? And that was different, wasn't it?

Many Americans, even comfortably off Californians, did not have access to the universal healthcare that he, and Fiona, and other Europeans, enjoyed almost as a birthright. They could not afford it. It was simply too expensive, and so they found an alternative.

The counter-culture of sixties California offered alternatives to pretty much everything that had gone before, and everything that their parents had always accepted unquestioningly. Colourful, vibrant, alternatives to the dull consumerist conformity of their parents' lives.

A whole alternative lifestyle that, by the time of The Summer Of Love in 1967, had drawn more than a hundred thousand young people, Fiona's teenage mother among them, to San Francisco to live the hippy ideal.

There was alternative music, alternative literature, alternative poetry and alternative painting. In free love, there was an alternative to monogamy. In peace, there was a universally attractive alternative to war, especially and urgently to the war in Vietnam.

In the widespread use of hallucinogenic drugs, there was even an alternative to reality. As was said at the time, reality is for those who can't cope with drugs.

Alternative medicine was not then, yet, much of a hippy thing, and it was not quite either yet the same thing as wellness, but the two shared roots, and they were roots that grew well in the flower children's rejection of consumerism and in their embrace of the spiritual.

And, perhaps most significantly, in the light of what followed then, and would again follow now, in their deeply held suspicion of government and authority.

Frank could not have been more than two years old when he first heard "San Francisco (Be Sure To Wear Flowers In Your Hair)" drifting from the neighbour's open upstairs window as Bill put him to bed one Summer Sunday evening in the terraced house in Irvine. But he remembered, if not the moment, then the song, to this day.

For some reason, it was the bridge that stuck in Frank's mind, though obviously, a two-year-old would have not known that it was the bridge. Nor would he have understood a word of what any of it meant.

Comprehension must have come later, it was a song that was played on the radio every summer, after all. But whenever, and however, it had come, there was something about it that had stayed with him, and that appealed to him.

San Francisco charted at Number 1 in the United Kingdom and enjoyed similar success in much of Europe. In the United States, where it had been released to promote the Monterey Pop Festival that was being organised by its writer, John Phillips of The Mamas & The Papas, it reached number 4 on the Billboard Hot 100 and remained there for a month. It eventually sold more than seven million copies.

Alternative medicine, and wellness, would take another generation to flourish, but what had begun life as alternative music was big business, and as such, it was instantly, and welcomingly absorbed into the mainstream.

Frank came to Bob Dylan and to Leonard Cohen, neither of whom ever thought of themselves as hippies in any case, late in their careers. He never really got Neil Young at all, though that was as much to do with the sound of his voice as anything else.

All the same, Frank found the 'stick it to the man' ethos of the few adolescent longhairs among the sixth form of Irvine Royal Academy to be affected, absurd, childish even.

Glasgow University had always been a deeply conservative seat of learning. Most undergraduates lived at home with their parents.

They were mostly studying to be doctors or lawyers or accountants, trainee or mini-me incarnations of 'the man' himself and so unlikely to be much interested in sticking it to themselves.

There were one or two dope smokers among the sociologists, but beer and whisky remained the stimulants of choice for the overwhelming majority of Frank's peers and Frank himself. He disliked the lack of focus that he found when smoking weed.

In those days, at least, young people in the west of Scotland generally preferred not to waste their time and money on stimulants that made them calm or sedentary, or in any way contemplative.

Heroin and Trainspotting were not to come till later, much later.

Then there was the climate and its impact on hippy fashion. The colours and the textures of tidye t-shirts, beads or flares never really did much to compliment woollen cardigans and practical rainwear. All in all, Kelvin Grove was always a long way from Laurel Canyon.

Frank, for all his subsequent travels and all of his later acquired worldliness, never really had much experience, nor ever showed any great interest, in anything in any way alternative.

Even now, thirty years later, before the thought and effort that he was now finding himself having to apply to it, it would be fair to say that his opinion of wellness was that it was, well, probably, at best harmless.

Unless, of course, you were daft enough to drink unfiltered rainwater, say, or to stick a jade egg in your vagina. A practice that even Fiona refused to take seriously.

That was not to say that Frank was unaware that Big Pharma, nothing less than 'the man' incarnate to the wellness community, had ever done anything much to endear itself to anyone other than its stockholders.

Even if that meant flooding vulnerable communities with addictive opiates, as eventually, it did.

But, if it was true that drug companies were more concerned with exploiting sickness than promoting health, then it seemed to Frank that it was equally true that wellness was as much about apportioning blame to others as it was about taking responsibility for yourself.

And, of course, he knew where that ended up.

Those dying of the virus were already sick, or they were old, or both, or else they had committed the worst sin of all, they were overweight.

Alternative medicine was not slow to offer alternative cures to such irresponsible unfortunates.

According to no less an authority than The President Of The United States Of America himself, the virus could easily be cured simply by drinking bleach.

These were strange days, but there were stranger ones to come.

Counter-culture to cancel culture. Perhaps Frank had not been entirely fair to avocados, or to Neil Young, for that matter.

To be fair to Fiona, she was not yet entirely comfortable on the wilder shores of what was known, far too flatteringly, Frank thought, as conspiracy theory.

The term, he believed, conferred an undeserved veneer of academic respectability on the clowns who promoted it. Surely it also protected them from the criminal prosecution that anyone practising such conspiracies would have naturally been subject to.

But he said nothing, at least not to Fiona. It was sufficient, for the present, for him to employ a strategy of containment.

He had known for some time now that there was little point in engaging in a reasoned argument with her, so he was careful neither to agree nor to disagree. This was to prove a mistake. Had he given the matter a fraction of the attention that he should have then he would soon have realised the obvious and chilling paradox. This stuff was in her blood.

He began to spend more time at Rue Tenbosch. And there he began to spend more time with Izidora, virtually, of course, if not always entirely virtuously. She was in Zagreb with her daughter, staying with her parents. Her husband had joined them.

Philippe was Belgian, a librarian, and an outwardly quiet and studious man, if no great intellectual. He was an adventurer, a keen hiker, a mountaineer, and a snowboarder. An outdoorsman librarian, if you will, whom Frank now thought it amusing to think of, if not ever to refer to in front of Izidora, as Conan The Librarian.

It still puzzled him how Izidora could have married such a man. Still, there were plenty who found him and Fiona an odd couple. Opposites, they say, attract.

Philippe had always been a fitness fanatic, but he had now become obsessive about his diet, and Izidora's, and Ana's, and her parents. He spent all day watching Youtube Videos.

He refused to wear a mask and had been cautioned twice by the police. A third offence, he had been warned, would result in his arrest.

He told Izidora that those dying of the virus were already sick, old, or overweight, or did not look after themselves. The virus was not causing excess deaths.

He told her to wake up. He argued with her parents. Her father had told her that he wanted him to leave. They had a small place on the coast that he could go to, but he would not leave without Ana, and neither Izidora nor her parents would let her go with him.

Izidora was crying now. Frank wanted to reach through the screen and hold her in his arms, but he could not. He wanted to kiss her, but he could not. He wanted to tell her that it would be ok, but he could not.

Because he knew that it would not.

# 20. Please Like And Share

Frank opened the Youtube link. Twenty-six minutes was brief by the standards of what Fiona considered to be essential viewing these days, but at least this one was in English.

So he made himself a cup of coffee and he lit a cigarette. He sat down at his desk in the small second bedroom that now served as his office in the apartment in Rue Tenbosch and he expanded the thumbnail to occupy the full screen of his desktop. He pressed play.

And he watched Plandemic: The Hidden Agenda Behind Covid-19, from start to finish. It was an interview with Judy Mikovitz, an American Research Scientist, by a Hollywood Documentary Film Producer called Mikki Willis. Both, at first sight, seemed plausible enough.

Over footage of a night time police raid on a suburban home, Mikovitz told the story of her arrest and her incarceration whilst she was working at The University of Nevada. She said that the US National Institute Of Allergy and Infectious Diseases, and its Director, Anthony Fauci, had bribed investigators in the case, and that, together with the US Department of Health and Human Services, they had 'colluded, and destroyed' her reputation as a scientist.

The dramatic music score, the tense, brooding atmosphere, the moody cinematography, all familiar devices of documentary films had the effect, as they were intended to, of making her story appear convincing. But Frank found himself a bit bored by it. It all seemed a bit 'so what' so far. But what was about to come would certainly make him, well, wake up.

As Mikovitz warmed to her subject, she stated: "wearing a face mask activates your own virus which makes you sick from your own reactivated coronavirus expressions."

There are "healing microbes" in saltwater and "sequences' in sand that can protect you against COVID-19, and beaches should therefore be re-opened immediately.

That there is evidence that the epidemic in Italy is linked to flu vaccines and the presence of coronaviruses in dogs, that flu vaccines contain coronaviruses, and that taking a flu vaccine increases your chance of contracting COVID-19 "by 36%."

That COVID-19 had been created "between, Fort Detrick, the US Army

Medical Research Institute of Infectious Diseases, and the Wuhan laboratory."

That "US hospitals were receiving cash bonuses for each patient death that they record as COVID-19. And that as a result, COVID-19 is being deliberately misreported and overstated in order "to control people."

That hydroxychloraquine, a widely available and inexpensive antimalarial drug, is an "effective" treatment. Fiona had talked about hydroxychloraquine, she had bought an organic form of it and was taking it. She had offered it to Frank who, consistent with his strategy of containment, had neither refused it nor taken it.

Fiona talked about Bill Gates also, and here was this Mikovits woman, as Frank could only now think of her, slyly repeating the same completely unfounded allegation that he was involved in causing the pandemic to profit from the development of a vaccine.

And then it was over. Frank closed the link and made himself another cup of coffee. And he lit another cigarette, and then another, and then he Googled first Judy Mikovitz and then Plandemic.

Surprisingly, one thing that she had said was true, or at least partially true, US hospitals were receiving cash bonuses for registering patient deaths as Covid-19. Though there was no evidence that this was causing any overstatement. If anything it was likely that US deaths, like those elsewhere, were most probably being underreported.

There was no evidence to be found for any other statement that had been made. Every word of it was nonsense.

Mikovitz had been charged with theft from her employer and the charges were subsequently dropped. A fact that she would later admit had left her "confused" over the ten years since the incident, and one that she would "try to learn to say differently."

Willis agreed to answer a series of questions tabled by journalists and "to be involved in civil discussions with doctors on all sides." He did neither.

Meanwhile, for every viewer like Frank, who took ten minutes on Google to fact-check Plandemic's content, there were a thousand more, like Fiona, who did not.

Instead, they liked and shared the link two and a half million times on Facebook alone in the first few days that it was posted. Spreading it, faster and further than the virus itself, until it had been viewed eight million times that week on Facebook, Youtube, Twitter and Instagram.

Generating more, and still more, of the same, and worse, as the sluice gates opened wide to release an inexorable, relentless tide of social media sewage.

That is what Frank called it, for that is what it was.

A tide that, within a few months, would come to engulf Europe's cities, Brussels included, in violent protest, and sweep America to the brink of a Coup D'Etat.

An understandable narrative of blame, perhaps, in a climate of fear, but one that was not a drawing of what was there, but a drawing of what was not there. Not an accurate representation, but a deliberate misrepresentation, devoid of specification and tolerance, and formed instead from implication and intolerance.

Copied and shared, algorithmically now, to the fearful and the credulous the world over, at the touch of a screen, to maintain a lie.

A map of the implausible and the impossible, it was utterly destructive, and yet, at the same time, brilliantly communicative.

What any of it had to do with wellness, God alone knows. For Frank certainly did not, and he wondered if Fiona did either. And, if she did, then how she could explain to him, to anyone, how it had come to this, how beauty had vanished before their eyes as meaning bled away to nothing.

Theoretically, it was Frank's work to combat, or at least to respond to this sort of stuff. To communicate with citizens, but in reality, he found little interest in such a mission, even one with a lowercase m. And less support, Eder was in Vienna and did not answer Frank's mails or return his calls.

But despite his newfound, and unwelcome, status as a third-country national, he was still receiving his salary and so, he assumed, he remained in employment.

Renaud was at his holiday home in Ile de Re. And, having now reverted to type since the election campaign, which in Renaud's mind had entirely vindicated all things social, he was not about to say, far less do, anything in any way critical of Facebook or Google.

Frank's unit had, understandably, interpreted the instruction to work from home as literally as possible, and now did what little they could get away with, which was as close to nothing as made no difference, virtually from anywhere but Brussels.

And who could blame them? They were young, and the only reason that they had relocated to Brussels in the first place was to work in an office which was now to remain closed to all but essential personnel until January.

They were not essential personnel, and neither was he, nor Renaud, nor even Eder.

So much for the war for our shared democratic values as Europeans. But that had been about Brexit, a battle for the survival of institutions, not about COVID, a battle for the survival of, well, a battle for survival.

And though the Brexit battle had now finally been lost, the institutions had survived. And nobody, not even Frank, had lost their job.

Health was not an EU competence, nor as the Frank of old would have put it, not even an EU incompetence. But surely it was an opportunity, a once-in-a-lifetime opportunity even, to demonstrate the much-vaunted solidarity that lay at its heart.

To show the real-life impact that its institutions can have on its citizens. To demonstrate their agility and flexibility to come together to take swift and effective action.

It was an opportunity for all of these things and more. It was very much a European story. And it was very far from being an Anglo-Saxon problem. But for all that it was not an opportunity that was taken.

The new Frank felt the old Frank returning. And that made him uncomfortable. He had been quietly proud of the fact that he had found himself able to cast off the weary cynicism that had dogged his career since its start.

For what is cynicism but the opposite of love, or at least its absence?

And yet, even as he began to feel the absence of Fiona's love and the cynic in him return, he found himself missing his Lait Russe in the cafeteria, and his cigarette on the terrace.

Some days he even found himself missing the lurking presence of Renaud. And the pleasure of imagining his demise as he hurled him onto the railway tracks.

And, although they now seemed to be seeing each other almost every other day, he found himself missing Izidora. He found himself worrying about her, and about Ana.

As much, if not maybe more, as he found himself worrying about Fiona. And about Gabriel, whom he had not seen now for a month or more.

He was not, however, missing Peppa who seemed to have included him in her bubble, though fortunately not among her knuffelvrienden, without either asking him or telling him. It was becoming harder to avoid her invitations to supper, and impossible to ignore her regular unannounced appearances at his door.

The fact that the mice in Rue Tenbosch had now been joined by rats was a matter of growing concern to her, in fact, it was becoming an obsession. And now that pretty much everyone else in their building had left town, being mostly, like Frank's colleagues, young Eurocrats with other options, she had nobody else to share it with but Frank.

That the closure of restaurants had caused the neighbourhood's rodent community to eat at home like everyone else was entirely logical if you thought about it. It was something that Frank had explained to her on more than one occasion, but still, the doorbell rang.

He was not missing the links that still arrived from Fiona two or three times a day. The links that came with her still kind, affectionate, and sometimes even still reasonable mails. But as the final weeks of that first confinement passed, they saw each other less and less.

When they did so, it was no longer in her apartment in Ste. Catherine nor in his on Rue Tenbosch, but to walk together in the Bois de La Cambre or the Parc Tenbosch.

There she was less likely to be stopped by the police, and so less able to use the opportunity to embarrass Frank by producing her doctor's exemption and ranting, there was no other, and certainly no polite, way of putting it now, about the need for everyone to wake up.

A habit, as Frank was now tired of reminding her, that would one day come to embarrass her more than him, if she were ever forgetful, or stupid enough, to light a cigarette mid-rant and find herself bundled into the back of a police van.

Since the Plandemic, and its sequel, which Frank was disappointed to find was not titled Plandemic II, but what he considered to be the rather lame pun: Plandemic: Indoctrination, the links that she sent were now mostly in French.

Consequently, conditional clause was piled upon conditional clause, and they took a very long time to make whatever point it was that they were trying to make. Given the volume of them that he was now receiving, Frank now watched few, if any, to the end.

The fact that he still watched any of them at all was not just down to his lingering loyalty to Fiona, but the fact that he still loved her. Though they no longer now made love. A loss that both regretted and that both accepted responsibility for.

As Frank felt Fiona evaporate, he felt Izidora condense around him.

He did not like either feeling, he wanted to go back to normality. He wanted to take Fiona to Scotland, he wanted to retrace their steps. He wanted them to take Gabriel and to sit together on the beach in Troon, as she had wanted once.

He wanted them to walk on the sand and to swim in the sea. Small pleasures, he thought, of which even Judy Mikovitz would surely approve.

But normality did not look like it would be an option for them, or for anyone else, any time soon. And besides, what if, as Fiona still kept telling him, it was normality that had caused this whole thing in the first place?

Izidora separated from Philippe. He returned to Brussels, to work, and fight for their freedom.
And for the rest of the summer, she remained in Croatia on the coast with Ana.

## 21. Fia

There was, Frank now discovered, a word for what Fiona had become.
Conspiritualism had been around since long before Plandemic, or even
the pandemic, though COVID-19 was what had, undoubtedly, now
caused the previously niche condition to spread so widely. It was, as Frank
had managed to figure out for himself, and, as the term itself suggested, a
coming together of spiritualism and conspiracy theory.

Fiona was a conspiritualist, there could be no doubt about that at all now.
And she was vanishing from view, as the gathering tide carried her further
and further from dry land, no longer waving, but drowning.

She was now so far out to sea that by the time that the first lockdown had
been finally, at least partially, lifted, she no longer answered to the name
Fiona at all.

Rationalising that the middle letters of Fiona were an inversion of the word
no, she had rechristened herself with the anagram, No Fia. Numerology
had something to do with it too, though what exactly remained unclear.

On social media, by way of explanation, or at least emphasis, she added
the conspiritualist mantra: Fear Is The Disease. Truth Is The Cure.

In real life, not that that was a place where she now spent much time, she
was simply Fia.

Perhaps, Frank thought, it was possible that at last she finally knew who
she was, perhaps not.

It was Friday night, and the sun shone, and Frank found it hard to believe
that it had only been twelve weeks since it had all begun, since the night
at Chez Martine with their friends, and the whisky and Auld Lang Sine.

Twelve weeks since they had staggered home together, and he had undressed her, caressed the perfect skin of her perfect body, held her in his
arms, and told himself that they would be ok, twelve weeks, and yet, also
a lifetime.

She had agreed to meet him for a drink, in fact, it had been her who had
suggested it, on the terrace of Au Laboureur. The interiors of bars and
restaurants were still closed and face masks were still mandatory when
not seated.

Most bars in the city now boasted extensive new terraces, hastily con-
structed out of wood, in the street. There was generally little traffic on the

Rue de Flandre so this was not too much of a problem there. But in Ixelles, and other parts of the city, some streets were now so restricted by new terraces that buses struggled to pass, and traffic slowed to a crawl.

It was a typically Belgian compromise, but for now, whilst most people continued to work from home, and did not have much need to get around the city, it worked well. It allowed bars and restaurants to reopen, and to begin to recoup some of their lockdown losses.

On terraces, table service was permitted till ten o'clock in the evening to groups of four people, provided that they remained seated and at least one metre apart at all times.

The rules were overelaborate, even the police agreed, even by Belgian standards. They would prove to be unenforceable, and it was not inconceivable that was the intention so that the police could eventually give up trying to enforce them.

But tonight, the first night of the unlocking, they were out on patrol, occasionally, randomly, asking people to sit down or to move tables apart, or put their face masks back on.

Space anywhere was at a premium, and since it was not permitted to drink standing up or to move between tables, Au Laboureur's already long-established, extensive, and sunny pavement terrace, found itself better suited than Chez Martine, for example, to life post lockdown.

Or life between lockdowns, as it was to prove to be.

Fia arrived late and she did not stay long. Long enough though for her to be cautioned for drinking while standing, moving between tables, and not wearing a face mask.

The doctor's exemption tonight elicited no more than an eye roll and a shaking of the head from a young policewoman who had encountered Fiona before and was now no longer buying any of it. She sat down and accepted Frank's offer of a face mask. But she did not put it on.

She told Frank that she was short of money and behind on her rent. Fiona had had little work, and now Fia had none at all. Telling her employers that they needed to wake up had probably not helped, Frank imagined.

But he said nothing, Nor did he mention her change of identity, though he had heard her give her name to the policewoman as Fia.

Nor about how she was dressed, in a military-style parka coat, over leggings and a jumper, an old pair of trainers on her feet.

Nor about, despite everything, how breathtakingly beautiful he still found her.

He quietly slipped her two hundred euro and he told her once again that he would not see her and Gabriel starve. She thanked him, and she kissed him once on his left cheek.

She did not inhale.

And then she was gone. Gone to meet friends at a bar in St. Gilles, she said. They were people that Frank did not know, but they were, apparently, awake. God, how Frank hated that word. God, how he wished that she would not wake up but shut up.

It was clear that even had he wished to, which he had not, he was not welcome to join her. And as those around him celebrated their newfound freedom, a sadness came to him, a sadness that hehad long known was coming, but one, nonetheless, that he was still not entirely ready for.

And he thought to himself how quickly love turns, not to hate, but to indifference, and how that's always somehow even harder to take.

And after she had gone, more than one of her old friends, their old friends, came and sat with him, and more than one of them bought him a beer, and more than one of them asked "Is Fiona ok?" And he told them: "that was not Fiona."

And he knew now, finally, that, despite all of his efforts, the strategy of containment had failed, and that it had failed dismally, and utterly.

But he knew also that this was not the end of the affair.

And that there was more, and worse, to come.

## 22. Hallelujah

By the end of the summer, COVID was back, and it was beginning to spread again. Mutating into new, more contagious, and more deadly variants, The Kent, the South African, and the Indian, all later to be changed to letters of the Greek alphabet to better disguise their origins, or at least where they had first been diagnosed.

In Belgium, the numbers were now as bad as they had been in the spring when the first lockdown was imposed, and they were getting worse. Some of this, it was said, was due to Belgium's practice of including all deaths where COVID was suspected as a factor, even if it had not been tested for, in the total.

Einstein put it well, and Frank had always been fond of quoting him, not least to Renaud and Eder in the context of social media and its reliance on vanity metrics. Not everything that can be counted, counts, and not everything that counts can be counted.

League tables of death had now become commonplace in the press, and especially in the British press, where the government's slow and confused response to the pandemic was now being excused by comparison to the worst affected EU member states. Oh Brexit, where is thy sting?

Izidora returned to Brussels with Ana in September. Philippe had moved in with Renaud, from where Frank assumed, he was now sending the text messages that he had begun to receive.

They were in English but misspelt, and they were sent late at night, when presumably he, and likely Renaud with him, had been drinking. Usually Frank did not see them until the morning.

They were not pleasant messages to wake to, but at first, they were at least brief, one-line warnings to stay away from his wife.

At first Frank ignored them. But as they became longer, and more unhinged, and began to refer to him and Izidora as 'being on the train to Auschwitz together' he told Izidora, and they stopped.

From time to time Frank still met with Fiona, or Fia, as she now insisted that he call her, or the Indian Variant, as he now thought of her, surprising himself at his ability to still allow a spark of humour to illuminate the darkness. Well, if you didn't laugh, you'd cry as Bill used to say.

They walked together in the Bois de La Cambre, usually making two or three circuits of the lake, depending on her mood, and depending on the degree to which Frank felt strong enough to listen.

Autumn, Frank often thought, was the season when Brussels was at its very best. It was usually mild and comparatively dry, and this autumn particularly so.

Sometimes, between circuits, they would stop beneath the slowly self-gilding trees to eat a Croque Monsieur together, or to share a coffee, or a Zinne Bir.

Sometimes Frank found that with patience and persistence he could manage to steer the conversation onto other, lighter, topics, at least for a moment or two.

He asked about Gabriel, and he told her to be sure to say hello to him. She asked after friends. And they reminded each other of things that they had done together, of meals that they had shared, and of places they had been together.

Sometimes he made her laugh. And sometimes he almost thought that he could detect some small, faint, echo of Fiona, the woman he had known, the woman who he had loved, and the woman who had loved him.

And sometimes, like today, he even allowed himself the hope that maybe, one day, reason might yet prevail. And that, one day, Fiona might return, if not to him, then maybe at least to reality.

But these were rare and fleeting moments in his deepening darkness and despair.

Fia, by contrast, he found to be optimistic and energetic, almost cheerful, almost as though the worse things became, and the more people died, the more she was vindicated.

She was certainly nothing if not engaged. Her engagement enraged him, it was another of those words, like awake, that had come to grate whenever it passed her lips, as both of them now did with monotonous regularity.

Truth was another one. The virus itself was harmless. Fear is the disease, truth is the cure. The claims of Plandemic now seemed almost harmless, innocent even, in comparison with what she now claimed as the truth and the cure.

COVID was the work of a global deep state run by a satanist cabal of paedophiles and child traffickers who numbered Bill Gates, of course, as well as Hillary Clinton, Bill did not seem to be mentioned for some reason, The Obamas, Hollywood, George Soros, and Queen Elizabeth II, who was also apparently a bloodsucking alien lizard, among their number.

The detail about the vampiric outer space reptilian origins of The British Royal Family was a long-held belief of a man called David Icke, who had once been a footballer and then a sports commentator on British TV. Frank was familiar with him from his childhood, but, as much as anything could surprise him these days, he was astonished to discover that, not only had the pandemic now granted him a renewed currency and credibility but that Fiona considered him to be a source of wisdom and authority.

Perhaps there was truth after all in the saying that gurus are for people who can't spell charlatan.

Only Donald Trump, Edward Kennedy, the US Military, and Vladimir Putin stood against them. The survival of humanity rested in their hands. And in the hands of the anonymous Q, who communicated with the resistance, Fia among them, in coded messages.

The development, and transmission of the virus, whether by 5G masts, or the contrails of aeroplanes, that detail no longer seemed important, was only the first part of the plan.

Its purpose was to serve as the excuse to allow a poisonous vaccine, possibly manufactured from the blood of abused children, though that detail was also unclear, to be administered, by force if necessary, to those who remained asleep.

Those who, like Frank, despite all his education, and however many degrees he had to his name, were just too stupid to be able to wake up. To do their own research, and to see the evidence all around them. And then to join Fia and bring down the system.

The deep state's goal was as simple as was sinister. The purpose of the vaccine was to achieve their long-planned ambition of a global genocide that would eliminate some eighty per cent of the world's population.

There were two vaccines apparently. The fatal one, and a harmless placebo one that was being administered to the twenty per cent who had been selected for survival as docile servants under the paedophile satanist cabal's total and unquestioned control.

The vaccine would not kill immediately, of course, that would attract suspicion, and the deep state was far too smart to do that. It would take many years, and the resulting deaths would be explained away by the constant invention of new and ever-evolving, but all entirely bogus, mutations of COVID.

It took several afternoons, and many circuits of the lake for Fia to explain all this as coherently, if that was the word, as Frank now understood it, or thought he understood it. The story was not always entirely the same, but that was the gist of it anyway.

Taking the vaccine, Fia told him, would be like getting on the train to

Auschwitz. He shuddered when he heard the comparison again. But he said nothing, perhaps because he had expected to hear it again, and to hear it from her lips.

Instead, he tried, as they made their third circuit of the lake that last afternoon, to point out at least a couple of the logical inconsistencies in all of this. How could it possibly be in the interests of global capitalism to kill eighty per cent of the world's consumers?

And surely the execution, no pun intended, of such a plan would require the close cooperation, the collusion in fact, of every country on Earth? The US, Russia, China, the EU, Iran and North Korea, to name but a few, all working together as one.

When no two of them had ever before in history agreed on anything that even allowed them to sell tomatoes to one another.

But Fia simply would not listen because Fia simply could not listen. It was now her first and foremost article of faith to reject out of hand any and every product of any form of informed or educated opinion.

To dismiss, without consideration, any proven scientific fact, and to rubbish any testimony of any expert or scientist, except the disaffected or the discredited. Judy Mikovits and David Icke, for example, or the entirely fictitious Swiss biologist, Dr Wilson Edwards, created by the Chinese with the sole aim of discrediting the WHO.

Perhaps at least this part of the faith, Frank thought, had its origins back in the sixties and The Summer Of Love and the 'whole generation with a new explanation' who even then, had held government and authority in deep suspicion. Yes, that part probably was in her blood.

But the other part of it, was it maybe even the more dangerous part he wondered, before concluding that there was probably really not much between the two, the part about doing your own research and seeing the evidence all around you.

That seemed to him less easily explained by hippies or history. And more likely to have come from conspiracist paranoia than from spiritual well-being.

Governments and corporations lie, that much Frank knew. In his heart of hearts, he admitted, there were times when he had helped them to do so.

But the idea that they were doing so on behalf of a deep state paedophile satanist cabal, well, as Fiona herself would say, do your own research, as he did, daily, and yet still he could find no evidence of it at all anywhere.

Yes, of course, there was big media, just like there was big Pharma, and yes, of course, Fox and Murdoch were not to be trusted, even if Fox seemed more and more each day to be taking her side of the argument, or

Trump's side of the argument anyway.

And it hit him then, as he said that, that Fia and Trump were on the same side. Bad men, and bad women, and good men, and good women, who do nothing. Authoritarianism is nothing if not inclusive.

But they were not controlled by governments. For one thing, Frank had plenty of colleagues, Eder included, who dearly wished that they were. And for another, it was true, then surely it was the other way around. And what of social media, you could hardly get more mainstream than social media, and yet they still seemed to get a free pass in all of this.

Uncontrolled, and uncontrollable by anybody, least of all governments, they were free to spread whatever sewage their ever-mutating algorithms determined best served their business model. As the English said, of another revolution in another age: 'Where there's muck, there's brass.'

They left the park as darkness fell. Fiona happily mask-less and Frank, pleased, or at any rate relieved, to have finally been able to have his day in court. His head was spinning, but at least henow understood her.

They walked, socially distanced, and now as ideologically, philosophically and emotionally distant as two human beings can be, down Chaussee de Waterloo, past Bascule, and on towards Rue Tenbosch. As they did so, Frank heard Leonard Cohen.

It was some time before Fiona interrupted the man with the gift of the golden voice.

Her money problems were now acute. Geert had stopped paying her any maintenance at all. He was starting to make noises about challenging the joint custody agreement.

The small Droit de passerelle, the welfare payment, which she had been receiving during lockdown had stopped. She was two months behind on her rent.

Frank knew what needed to be done. "Come in for a coffee," he said.

He found himself surprised by the ready acceptance of the invitation. But not at all by the fact that once she had removed her coat and her trainers, and now that she was settled at the table, she suggested that they should instead take a glass of red wine.

Nor by the fact that already assuming his answer, it was her who took two glasses from the cupboard, and the already open bottle of Montepulciano from the sideboard.

"You make yourself at home," Frank said. And she smiled. It was good to see her smile."You wish" she said and she took a pouch of tobacco and a packet of cigarette papers from her bag.

Frank went through to the bedroom, leaving the door open, more out of habit than by way of invitation. And he returned with the shortbread tin.

In his brief absence, she had poured two glasses of wine, found herself an ashtray, and lit the pair of candelabra that she had bought for him on their trip to Copenhagen.

And lit what Frank could now see, as well as smell, was not a roll-up, but a joint. She took a taff, as she called it, inhaled, and passed it to him.

He passed the shortbread tin across the table to her and she opened it. And although he was far from a habitual dope smoker himself, and forgetting, or perhaps ignoring, the risk of infection in sharing a joint, he also took a taff, inhaling deeply.

"Don't spend it all at once" he said. "And try and keep as much of it in Sterling for as long as you can, it'll do better than the Euro, at least until this is all over."

And then they both stood up, almost as though the wine and the candlelight and the shortbread tin had somehow combined to confer a sense of celebration on the occasion. Or else a sense of occasion on the celebration. Almost as though it was Christmas or a birthday, and the shortbread tin was but the first of many presents that they would exchange.

She hugged him tightly and she held him in her arms. "You're a good man Frank," she said. "In fact, I think that maybe you were the absolute very best ever."

A tear came to her eye. "And I'll always love you, you know that." She took a drink and Frank passed the joint back to her. "Even if you are wrong about everything".

And Frank knew then that she was finally gone. He was old enough and wise enough to know that when a lover tells you that she will always love you then you may be certain that there are no circumstances in which they will ever sleep with you again.

A tear came to his eye also. And he knew that Fiona was irreplaceable. Fia was irrational, irresponsible, and irritating beyond words, but Fiona was irreplaceable.

A weight fell from his shoulders, he felt relief. For the sadness, and there was a deep, deep sadness in his heart, had already been, what is it they say, priced in. He would be ok. And she would be ok too.

Brussels locked down again two weeks later.

## 23. Izidora

"Why not? You always used to talk about killing Renaud". She slid the black silk bra strap from her shoulder. "Back in the days when you never smiled."

Frank closed his lips around her nipple and caressed it with his tongue. Him and his big mouth. Kill her husband, no, that was something that he would certainly not be doing.

"You know he's gay" The words stopped Frank in his tracks. He raised his head from her breast and he looked up at her. "Renaud?" he asked, realising as he did so the answer that was to come.

She paused and then almost crying, she said, "And Philippe" She slid off the other strap and let her bra fall from her shoulders. "Don't stop, Frank."

"They were lovers, a long time ago, before I met him," Frank said nothing. He doubted that it would ever be possible for him to feel sorry for Renaud, but he certainly felt sorrow or something like it.

"Renaud thought you were too, at first."

Yes, sorrow and perhaps also even a little guilt. "You're a disappointment to him."

Why had she never told him? Why had she never told anyone?

He moved his mouth to her other breast and then slowly down her now naked body. She carried on talking "It took me a long time to figure it all out".

Calmly, almost matter of factly as she savoured the pleasure of Frank's mouth, of Franks's lips, of Frank's fingers on her, and in her.

"They're very good liars, both of them."

She had known Frank for twenty years now. And they had dated then. But Izi had never been what Frank thought of as one of his great romances. She was not, by her admission, one of the great romantics.

She had Doctorates in Philosophy and Linguistics. Her father, now retired, had been a poet of some celebrity in the former Yugoslavia.

Her mother was a judge and also a woman who considered herself to have some wisdom in affairs of the heart. She had distrusted Philippe long before the wedding.

And she had disliked him since long before they had been forced to lockdown together. She found his unwillingness, or inability, to ever attempt conversation with her or her family in anything but his native tongue, not just impolite and selfish, but suspicious.

She was a lawyer, after all, and she knew when people were hiding things. But she had always liked Frank. And her daughter's feelings for him had always been obvious to her. As obvious as the fact that Izi too was hiding something from her.

But she said nothing, biding her time in the knowledge that what would be would be.

Finally now taking her mother's advice 'to be sure and not let him slip through your fingers again' to heart, Izi held Frank's hands tightly in hers, her now long blonde hair brushing his face as she moved above him.

Her mother was not alone in having detected an air of unfinished business between them. The many colleagues and contemporaries who had long suspected that to be the case would be happy, if not to see them now, that would be voyeurism, then at least to know that they had been correct.

Izi pressed herself firmly into him, and then gently apart again.

Philippe and Renaud had been college friends, and she had never had reason then to think that they were anything more. Then, he had been a change from what was becoming a familiar routine and what she thought, a rather incestuous social scene of contemporaries at work and their friends from home, few of whom had jobs outside the Institutions.

She had met Frank too early and too young. And even in the year that they spent together, he had always seemed to be somehow detached, not just from her, but from life.

For Frank's part, he was in no doubt that in Izi he had found a woman who was not only his intellectual equal but in many ways a good deal smarter than him.

She was comfortable in her skin, grounded, sensible, practical, maybe a little too much so for him. And she was beautiful, short, a good half a metre shorter than him, with golden blonde hair which she wore cropped short, and green eyes. And cheekbones which Frank liked to tell her were sharp enough to open envelopes.

He had noticed her before he had even taken his seat that first morning at their first induction. He was not alone. Others had pursued her, but from among the many possibilities she had chosen Frank. The one who had not, or, at least, had not given the impression, of doing so.

The sex, which, despite the absence of firearms or airport lingerie, had always been good, but she had seemed to him then to be, a little, well, dull. No, that was unkind, not dull, and not boring either, but certainly a good deal more conservative than at least he considered himself to be.

She was not a party animal. She was easily bored by bars and socialising. She dressed conservatively, as if embarrassed, if not by her beauty, then by her attractiveness, her sexiness, her desirability. She had conservative tastes in music and movies. She was not afraid or embarrassed to admit to liking Coldplay or enjoying Love Actually.

Frank, being a man, and worse, an Anglo-Saxon man of a certain age, was the worst kind of snob in both regards. He considered Coldplay to be Radiohead for people who didn't read books, though he was, quietly fond of Bill Nighy's turn in Love Actually.

For the child of a poet and a judge, even a poet and a judge that had been born and raised as communists, the conservatism seemed odd. Yet she was well-read and well-travelled.

Was it not more likely closer to the truth that their relationship had been another occasion when he had not given the matter the thought that it deserved until it was too late?

That his customary caution, on the one, indeed the only, occasion that he had ever found himself with someone with whom he was entirely compatible, had led him to lack commitment. Rather than to the habitually impulsive over-commitment to someone entirely incompatible, like an armed criminal, or a deranged conspiritualist, for example.

But perhaps he was being too hard on himself. Most likely it was it bit of both, and a whole lot of other stuff too. Whatever the reason they had drifted apart and each had found others. Though there had been one more encounter since then.

It would have been an exaggeration to call what had happened an affair, or even a fling. It was after a Christmas party and they were both drunk, so far, so cliched. She had already been with Philippe for almost two years then, he had proposed marriage to her, but she had not accepted, and she was not entirely sure that she should or would. He had been with the Dutch girl at the time. Izidora fell pregnant with Ana and married Philippe soon after.

Of course she knew that it had been a mistake if only a minor one in the light of all that was still to come. But Frank remembered it clearly and fondly. There was something about sex with an ex-girlfriend. It was a cliche, perhaps, but cliches are cliches because they are true. It had been, in Frank's mind, and only in hindsight, of course, so completely wrong that it had been just right.

Not that it had ever been a regular or even occasional experience with anyone else. Now that he thought of it, it had been unique.

And now here they were again. But he knew that this was no one-night,

95

or one afternoon, stand.

He was committed now, a good deal more committed than he knew, in fact, as he found himself held in the rhythmic movement of her body, of her body and his together.

Yes, he was being too hard on himself. Wasn't it just the simple truth that he now found himself in a place where he felt a lot more comfortable with who he was? That that place was Izi's bed, well, perhaps that was just inevitable.

For her part, she certainly found him no less attractive now, and no less amusing. Quite the opposite now that he had at last grown into his age. Now that he no longer felt the need to cultivate his detachment, or to wear what remained of his cynicism quite so proudly.

They were one now, made so by the force of their desire for one another. A force that there was no longer any point in denying, even had either wished to.

In the light in her eyes he saw not the sadness of a love that was lost, but the joy of one that was found again.

She was four years younger than Frank and also an only child. They had followed similar academic paths, but although she rarely mentioned it, she had two more doctorates than he did.

Both were accomplished linguists, with eight languages between them, or nine if you counted Frank's attempts at Croat, the only few words of which he could ever remember he spoke with a Scottish accent, because it amused her, and also because it turned her on.

But there the similarities ended. Her parents had been sweethearts since their schooldays in Zagreb and both had always been high achievers.

Neither of them had ever been with anyone else, and after forty-six years of marriage they were both still completely devoted to one another, and to their daughter.

If ever a day passed when one or either was travelling and they could not see each other, then they spoke on the telephone. Izi could not have been brought up in a more loving household.

Frank was fond of describing Scotland in the seventies as 'like the Soviet Union, only with orange juice' but the reality was that the disintegrating war-torn Yugoslavia of her youth was a very far cry from the Scotland of his.

From what he knew of the history of The Balkans, Frank understood that, of course, but listening to Izi he realised that in reality, he knew nothing. And he found that to be humbling. She had been twelve when Marshal Tito died, and she remembered her parents wearing black.

Neither had ever been active party members, though their jobs required that they demonstrated their loyalty as and when it was required. All jobs did then, but theirs especially so. Her father's work was not censored. He was both too smart to court controversy and too well known to need to. The judiciary enjoyed a reasonable degree of independence.

As a child, Izi had never heard either of them speak a word against their country or its ruler.

Around the same time, within a week or two of Tito's death certainly, she remembered both of them sitting her down in her father's study. It must have been a Saturday or a Sunday because she was not at school, and they were not the kind of people who went to church.

She remembered the map on the wall of the study. And she remembered her father talking to her about nationality, ethnicity, and religion. Words that she struggled to understand that morning as much as she still did now.

She remembered his largely, though not entirely, accurate prediction of what was to come. For who could have entirely foreseen the scale of the horror that would unfold?

Ten years still had to pass, in growing acrimony and growing poverty too, before the Yugoslavian war, or wars finally broke out in Croatia. At the Battle of Borovo Selo where her father's brother, and his sixteen-year-old son, Izi's cousin Filip, died at the hands of Serbian militiamen.

Within the year she had graduated from the University of Zagreb and enrolled on her first Masters at Ankara University. But in the years that she then spent in Turkey, and Germany, and finally in Brussels, there would not be a person that she knew whose life was not touched by war.

If he was not quite the hero that he was in Bosnia, the fact that Tony Blair, and Bill Clinton also, remained popular in Croatia was still not something that Frank could entirely believe.

But the uselessness of the EU who, to their eternal shame, simply sat on their hands as her former countrymen died in their tens of thousands was a fact that he could not dispute.

That, she had told him, on the very first morning that they met, all those years ago, was the reason that she was here. And the reason that she chose to do the job that she did.

So it had been hope or, rather, belief, or faith even, that Frank had thought of as dullness. And he cursed himself now for that almost fatal misdiagnosis.

But wasn't that the problem with faith, and the point of it too? It only really worked if you believed in it.

It was not Izi that had been boring, but him, leaning as he had on whatever superficial social props he could find to hand. And isn't it usually the case that you only appear boring when youcan no longer be bored?

Ever since that Saturday morning in her father's study in Zagreb, she had known that it was an inevitability that the land of her birth would come to be torn apart.

And she had known also that it was an inevitability that she would eventually choose to come here, and choose to do this. To try, if she could, to stitch something of it together again.

Perhaps there was an inevitability also in the fact that she would find a time and a place to come together again with Frank. To stitch the two of them back together again, if she could.

But if there was an inevitability about this, then it came also with a note of caution.

A nota bene to the effect that, just as neither had escaped nor could ever escape, the scars of their upbringings, neither had escaped their other relationships entirely unscarred either.

Nor could they, for many of the less pleasant, and certainly most of the less believable, details of their oddly parallel experiences had been common, if not actually shared.

Both knew all too well that the rebound is where mistakes are often made, and where they are also often harder to unmake.

She released her grip on his hands. She leant forward on her elbows and stroked his hair. They kissed, and they kissed and they kissed.

And then she rested her face on his chest. "There's something that I want you to do, Frank," she said, "for me and for Ana."

He felt a teardrop roll from her eye onto his chest. And without asking, he knew already what it was. "Of course," he said.

## 24. Marching As To War

The first La Boum had originally been conceived as a Poisson d'Avril, an April Fool's joke. April Fool, like most forms of practical joke, is well suited to the French sense of humour, which, unlike English humour, or Dutch humour, usually likes to have a victim.

It was a free concert in the Bois de La Cambre, it was widely promoted on social media, and would, the organisers said, feature a headline set by Calvin Harris and a Daft Punk reunion show.

Or rather, it would not. The victims of the joke were the five thousand people who turned up on the day, all in breach of lockdown restrictions, only to be dispersed by the police.

Although not specifically organised as such, it was, after all, just a joke, La Boum attracted a young, and mostly anti-lockdown, and anti-vax crowd. Not that they were always the same people.

A schism was already developing in the resistance movement, as sooner or later, schisms invariably do in most resistance movements.

Fia went, of course, with her new circle of friends, and with a placard that she had spent a large part of the previous week designing and making herself, even enlisting Gabriel's help with its assembly.

Something that, had he been aware of it, would have caused Geert to do rather more than just make noises about the custody agreement.

It said simply and succinctly: 'Wake Up' in bold black type on a white background. It was widely admired that afternoon, and later again at La Boum 2.

Philippe was there too, and not only managed to get himself arrested, but to star on that evening's television news programmes while doing so. Several of which, in Belgium and beyond, ran footage of him throwing flares in what appeared to be the general direction of policemen in riot gear. And then, not unsurprisingly, being handcuffed and bundled into the back of a police van.

The incident earned him some celebrity among Fia and her new circle. And although the two newly self-styled light warriors of Frank's acquaintance were yet to meet in person, it would not be long now until they did. Izi did not watch the news that evening. But plenty of friends and colleagues did. And plenty of them shared it with her.

Along with their disapproval, and their concern, not least about Ana.

Eventually, of course, it reached Izi's mother in Zagreb who called her daughter immediately to remind her husband that their custody agreement for Ana was a voluntary arrangement between them and could, and would, be reviewed was he to cause the family any further embarrassment.

And so, the morning of La Boum 2 dawned. It was a week before Brussels was due to unlock again, after what had been another eight months of confinement.

You might then reasonably have asked the anti-lockdown schism why they felt the need to protest about something that they already knew perfectly well was going to happen next week anyway.

Though there would, of course, have been no point in asking the anti-vax schism anything at all.

Frank was still in bed with Izi at the apartment on Rue Tenbosch when Fia messaged him. The fact that she was on her way to the Bois de La Cambre was no surprise, but that she wanted to stop by for a coffee en route, if that was ok, was unexpected.

They had no contact, either real or virtual, since before Christmas.

There was not a jealous bone to be found anywhere in Izi's body, but she was still understandably unenthusiastic about welcoming Fiona as a guest in the apartment.

Frank agreed to meet her instead in the small garden in the square on Place Brugman. There they could once more share the most expensive takeaway coffee to be found anywhere in Brussels, from Voltaire, as they had often done before in other times.

Izi had some shopping to do anyway and said that she would maybe pass by later. She was curious to finally meet Fiona in the flesh, as it were. She would say hello and then see her off on her way, which was, Frank agreed, just exactly the perfect English idiom to describe what needed to be done.

Fiona was already there, seated on a bench under the trees, her placard resting on the bench opposite when Frank arrived. He had bought two lait russes and a couple of the almond croissants which had always been her favourite back in the day.

The placard was professionally designed, Frank would have expected no less. It was an impressive piece of carpentry and a sizeable one too. Its long wooden handle having been fashioned by Gabriel from a fence post purchased from Brico, Fia told him, with some pride.

Frank needed both hands, and most of his, admittedly not terribly impressive, strength to pick it up, and then raise it above his head, in a misjudged attempt at humour.

"I don't know about waking anyone up," he said, "but you could certainly put someone to sleep with this if you're not careful."

Fiona would have laughed, Fia did not, her sense of humour, Frank imagined, having been taken, along with her sense of reality, by the body snatchers when they had swapped her over with the replicant now sitting on the bench beside him.

Frank was not much of a sci-fi fan, but he had always liked the actor Donald Sutherland and he remembered enjoying his remake of Invasion Of The Body Snatchers at The Odeon in Irvine when he must only have been twelve or thirteen years old.

He could imagine an empty Fiona-shaped pod lying on the terrace of her apartment or else in the cellars of Chez Martine or Au Laboureur.

He asked after Gabriel, and he told Fiona to be sure to compliment him on his woodwork skills. They drank their coffees and they shared their almond croissants, on the subject of which Fiona did not comment at all. They small talked about nothing much in particular for what could only have been twenty minutes or so before Izi appeared across the street, though to Frank it felt longer.

She was talking with a girlfriend on her phone, or as she would later admit, she was doing a very convincing impression of someone who was pretending to talk with a girlfriend on her phone.

She did not look like she had been shopping. She looked like she had spent the last hour in hair and makeup. She wore a short dark blue summer dress and black heels. And she wore them well.

Fiona got up to hug her. But Izi neatly sidestepped the move and continued with her call for at least another minute, before ending it with an au revoir and a ciao and a kiss.

She apologised profusely for being so rude, she kissed Frank on the lips and ruffled his hair. And then, and only then, did she casually fist-bump Fiona. God, she's good at this shit, Frank thought.

Ever the diplomat, or ever the coward, perhaps, he walked slowly away from them across the small patch of grass. He put the coffee cups and the paper bag in the bin, lingering a little as he did so, taking care, and more time than was necessary, to make sure that he had stuffed them down firmly, and that they could not possibly escape.

This was all a good deal more awkward than he had thought that it would be, or feared that it could be. He felt distinctly uncomfortable, though Izi did not, nor did Fia.

"You're a lucky, woman, Isabel," she said. Frank felt something inside of him die a little. He knew there was worse to come, and it was barely a second before he was not disappointed.

"He's a good man. He's just a bit stupid." Izi looked at Frank and smiled. "Which is surprising for someone so smart." She said nothing. For she, of course, was nothing if not smart herself. A good deal smarter than Fiona, for sure. And far, far, too smart to bite on the bait.

"And he's wrong about everything." Frank looked at her "Fiona," he said, attempting to begin to bring the conversation to an end, and save himself, and her, from any further embarrassment.

"You'll see," she said, picking up her placard. "This afternoon, and all over the world too, not just here." She lifted it easily with one hand "Where is it you're from, Isabel?"

She swung it over her shoulder with an almost practised nonchalance. "Serbia?"

How long had Frank put up with this woman, Izi wondered, and why?

"There as well, Isabel, all over the world, people are waking up."

And leaving that thought, not so much hanging in the air, but rather ricocheting around the square, Fiona left taking Fia the light warrior, with her, thank God.

Off up past the elegant villas on the Rue Joseph Stallaert, marching as to war, to Vanderkindere, and then on, on to do battle with the deep state in the Bois de La Cambre.

"Jesus Christ, Frank" Izi sighed. She shook her head. "She's worse than Philippe."

"I worry about her," Frank said. "And with good cause, I think" Izi added. She took his arm. "Come on," she said. "Let's get some lunch, and then you, I think, have a doctor's appointment?" She kissed him. Frank smiled, but he said nothing. "Thank you," she said.

"Isabel, ok, get my name wrong if you must, but Serbia, fucking Serbia, for fuck's sake, Frank, what a fucking cow."

"She didn't mean it," Frank said. "Oh yes, she did. Sometimes you can be so naive. And don't defend her." They walked through the trees on Avenue Lepoutre and stopped at the pizzeria opposite The Toucan Brasserie.

## 25. If You Go Down To The Woods Today

There were noticeably fewer attendees today.

The morning sun had gone elsewhere, and it had started to rain, lightly, but steadily. And the antilockdown schism did seem to have had second thoughts.

There were noticeably more police too. And this time they were noticeably better prepared. They had brought a water cannon today, and there were more Police Federal among their number and fewer local bobbies, as Frank liked to call the cops from the Municipalite.

There were more of them in riot gear and more of them on horseback. This time they looked like they had come ready for a fight. And this time they did not look like they were in much of a mood to go home without one.

Fia had gathered a group around her on her march through the leafy bourgeois streets of Ixelles. They were all women, and all around her age, all devotees of wellness, and all dressed as though they were on their way to a yoga class.

One had brought along her two well-groomed, if rather overexcited, teenage children, but only after they had sworn not to tell their father, a judge, where their mother was taking them for the afternoon.

Another was a mother from Ana's school and she already seemed to know Philippe.

Fia recognised him immediately. He was by now something of a celebrity among the various anti-vax Facebook groups to which most of them seemed to belong. And Facebook still did nothing at all to moderate, far less to shut down or remove.

She introduced herself as a light warrior. "Me too." He smiled and kissed her once on each cheek. He smelled slightly of Ricard. "I'm Philippe."

He made much of admiring her placard and she offered to make one for him too. She liked the sound of his name. They exchanged numbers. "I'll call you when it's done, and you can maybe come over and have supper." She was flirting with him. And why not? There had not been a man in her bed since Frank.

That it was clear that the mother from Ana's school could see her intentions only encouraged her. Though she knew that Fia was wasting her time, she did not say so. She had herself only recently made the same mistake.

Philippe told Fia that he was a librarian and he asked her if she was English. She told him only that she was a child of the universe. It stopped raining. And an uneasy calm settled over the park.

The police repeated their loud hailer announcement in French, and then in Dutch, and then in German, and then also in English. Everyone present was in breach of lockdown regulations and they should all now leave the park and make their way home.

If not then they should expect to be arrested.

A woman in Fia's group, whom she had not met before this afternoon, began to argue that they had succeeded in making their protest and that they should now do as the police said. Another woman agreed, as did the teenage boy.

Philippe disagreed. Another woman suggested a compromise, whereby they would leave the park if a representative group were allowed to remain in a silent vigil for freedom and democracy.

Fiona disagreed. The discussion became heated. Schisms were now developing within the schism. It was all starting to sound a bit reminiscent of The Life Of Brian and The Judea People's Front, or was it People's Front of Judea? Or The Popular Front of Judea? Or the Judea People's Popular Front?

The rain started again, it was getting colder, and a wind was beginning to blow up the hill. Some of the group began to drift away. There were probably no more than a thousand of them left, matched, if not now probably outnumbered, by the police. More of them were now arriving in a convoy of white police vans with metal screens fixed across their windows.

The police made another announcement. This time it was an ultimatum. The protesters had twenty minutes to disperse and leave the park peacefully. Anyone remaining then would be arrested.

Force would be used if necessary.

More people drifted off, including everyone that Fia had arrived with. She and Philippe were now alone together.

Five minutes passed, and then ten, and then fifteen. The first police line moved slowly up the hill on foot. And then stopped. As good as their word, they would give the protesters the twenty minutes that they had said that they would.

Philippe took two flares from his rucksack. He handed one to Fia and lit the other.

From the mostly male group behind them, bottles began to fly over their heads towards the police line, who now charged forward up the hill, riot shields and batons held aloft.

Fifty or so protesters, dreadlocked anarchists to a man and a woman, ran down the hill to meet them. Philippe threw his flare, and then turned and started walking, calmly at first, as though he was out for a stroll, and had nothing to do with any of this, down the other side of the hill towards the exit from the park.

Fia turned and followed him, quietly dropping her unlit flare to the ground, but still firmly gripping her placard, as more police now appeared from the woods on either side of the hill, forcing the mostly fleeing protesters towards the water cannon which had been deployed, with a line of mounted police waiting behind it, to block the exit.

The water cannon waited until they were within range and then opened fire.

Over Philippe and Fia's heads at first, but now lower, at those in front of them, knocking them off their feet. Philippe was running now, trying to get in front of the jet of water.

Fia ran behind him, but he was running faster and she was losing ground on him. He turned around to try to look for her face in the crowd.

And as he did so, he lost his footing on the wet grass and fell heavily to the ground.

A jet of water hit Fia with full force directly in her stomach.

It lifted her body into the air, where she seemed to hang, defying gravity for a moment, before landing on top of Philippe.

It might have been the firmness of her grip, or it might have been the hard edge of the fencepost from Brico, or it might just have been its sheer weight, but whatever the reason, the placard's wooden handle struck a heavy blow to the back of Philippe's head.

There was no sign of blood. But there was no sign of life either.

The next thing that Fia remembered, perhaps she also lost consciousness for a moment or two, was the crackle of radios as two policemen bent over Philippe's body.

Fia went with him, and the two policemen, in the ambulance.

There was no pulse. The paramedic tried AED once, twice, and three times, but without success.

She was of Indian descent, and she took Fiona's hand as they slowly edged their way through the Saturday afternoon traffic, lights flashing, siren ablaze. "Miracles can happen," she said.

Philippe was pronounced dead on arrival and his body was taken to the morgue.

Izi was with Frank when she got the call from the hospital. He went with her in the taxi.

Nobody spoke. And it was only when the doctor reappeared and led Izi away to complete the formal identification of her husband's body, that Fia finally realised the awful truth, if not yet of what she had done, then, at least, of what had happened.

The swing doors swung closed.

"Oh, God," she said, stepping forward to embrace Frank. "It was an accident."

"He was her husband, and you..." but the next two words would not come. Although he knew them to be true.

"It was the police," she said. "The water cannon." Frank stepped back and away from her, avoiding her open arms.

"She should be proud, he was a warrior." Frank looked down at her mud-spattered leggings and trainers. Utterly unable to believe the stupidity, the self-importance, the egotism, the crassness, the heartlessness, the sheer mindless, twisted, repulsive bad taste of her words.

Thank God, Izi was not here to hear them. "And he died in battle," she said. Frank turned on his heels and stormed out of the building, incandescent in his impotent rage.

Fia did not follow him. Through the windows, he could see that she was talking to two policemen. He just hoped, for her sake, that she was not repeating what she had said to him. Or did he? Go on, he thought, go on and get yourself arrested. And locked up. You killed a man. With a weapon that you made with your child.

He lit a cigarette, and he tried to calm himself. He looked at his watch. And, as night fell, he waited to take Izi home with him.

## 26. A Person Of Interest

The interview was conducted in English. But for all the sense that it made to Frank, it might as well have been in Croat, or Mandarin Chinese.

It began pleasantly enough. The Inspector thanked Frank for coming into the station, and on a Sunday, to help the police with their enquiries.

When he entered the room, he had seemed to be shorter than Frank, but now that they sat opposite one another, he was looking down on him. Were the chairs of different heights?

He was around the same age as Frank with long, unkempt, and slightly greying hair. And stubble that was not quite a beard, but also not quite not a beard.

He wore jeans that had been ironed, and a black pullover over a white t-shirt. He was, Frank thought, trying a little bit too hard to look like a cop in a TV show.

He was Flemish, and he pronounced every word that he spoke slowly and deliberately. But still, not a single one of them made any sense whatsoever. He was from the Police Federal but he had not been present in the Bois de La Cambre yesterday, he told Frank. He said that Frank was not under arrest and that he was free to end the interview at any time that he wished to do so.

And why would I be under arrest? And what for? I wasn't present in the Bois de La Cambre yesterday, either. Frank thought but did not say.

Surely, even in Belgium, you have to do something to get arrested?

It was possible, however, perhaps even likely in the inspector's opinion, that he would be named as a person of interest in the enquiry into the death of Monsieur Malibran.

A person of interest was, he explained, just exactly that, no more and no less.

"So I would advise your full and, er, frank cooperation". The Inspector laughed at his little English joke.

"The first thing that we do in these circumstances, Mr McDonald."Is to look and see if we can establish some connection between the victim and his assailant."

"His assailant," Frank repeated. "Yes, the American woman, Madame Anderson". Frank took a moment before he realised that the Inspector meant

Fiona. "They were together at the demonstration yesterday, but they did not go there together. Madame Anderson met with you, and with Monsieur Malibran's estranged wife Madame Ludovic, on her way there, did she not?"

"She did," said Frank, "And as you are already aware, Inspector, I know both of them well."

"Indeed, we shall come to that, but they were not previously known to each other, Monsieur Malibran and Madame Anderson".

This was not a question, but a statement. Frank answered it anyway "Not so far as I know."

He found himself having to concentrate to remember just who these people that the Inspector insisted on referring to as Monsieur This and Madame That were. He had not slept well, in fact, he had hardly slept at all, but he thought it best to stick with the Inspector's choice of formalities.

"In the ambulance, she called him by name but their phone records show that their first contact was only two hours or so before Monsieur Malibran's death".

The Inspector had opened a file of typewritten notes, to which he now started to refer.

"So yes, I think we can agree at least that the victim and his assailant were not previously known to one another". Jesus, thought Frank, now we're back with the victim and his assailant again.

"And I think that we can also agree that your earlier meeting with Madame Anderson would probably be the most likely explanation for why your fingerprints are on the weapon used in the assault."

He paused. "The fatal assault, Mr McDonald."

His fingerprints? How the? He was in a police station. The Inspector had invited Frank to enter the room first, and it was Frank who had opened the door.

He heard Izi's voice in his head. "Sometimes you can be so naive."

"There was an argument?" The Inspector looked down at his notes again.

"No," said Frank, trying to fight his tiredness.

"Your girlfriend, Madame Ludovic, the victim's estranged wife, was heard to call the assailant, who is your former girlfriend, is she not? And I quote Madame Ludovic's words exactly if you'll forgive me, a fucking cow."

"Fiona had gone by then, Izi addressed those words to me, not to her, and I have never made any secret of the fact that, yes, Izi is my girlfriend, and that, yes, Fiona is a former girlfriend, a coincidence, Inspector, and nothing more."

"If, perhaps, an unfortunate one, in the circumstances, Mr McDonald, but please listen carefully to what I say. I said that is what Madame Ludovic was heard to call the assailant, I did not say that is what she was heard to say to the assailant."

"Ok," Frank nodded. "Thank you," the Inspector seemed to almost smirk. He was building his case, whatever it was, patiently, and it had to be said, also rather well.

Frank's tiredness was curdling into fear now with every slow, deliberate word that the Inspector spoke. Just where the fuck was this going? He tried to calm himself.

"It is another unfortunate coincidence, is it not, that the phone records also show your number to have been called, not only by the assailant, your former girlfriend but also by the victim, the estranged husband of your girlfriend."

But he could not calm himself, he was sweating, the fear becoming panic. "A man who, on several occasions, over several weeks, has been sending you messages warning you to stay away from his wife."

And the panic finally boiled over into anger.

"Oh, this is ridiculous." Frank had had enough of this now. "It doesn't make any sense".

"Crimes of passion, rarely do, Mr McDonald, that's why they're called crimes of passion, if they made sense, then they'd be called crimes of reason, wouldn't they?"

The Inspector smirked. Frank wanted to hit him but instead laughed. "This is not a laughing matter, Mr McDonald, a man is dead."

"And you think that I had something to do with that, is that what you're telling me?"

The question hung in the air, unanswered. The Inspector shuffled his notes.

"On the 15th of June of last year, you were cautioned at Edinburgh Airport boarding Ryanair Flight FR 7352 to Brussels. You were in possession of the sum of nine thousand, six hundred and forty pounds sterling in cash, concealed in a biscuit tin in your luggage."

"And what the fuck has that got to do with anything?"

"We're not on a TV show, Mr McDonald, moderate your language, please." Frank apologised and the Inspector carried on. "But yes, you're right, no offence was committed."

He looked down at his notes.

"And it would certainly have nothing whatsoever to do with this enquiry, were it not for the fact that Madame Anderson deposited precisely the same sum of money in pounds sterling in cash into her current account at the De Brouckere Agency of BNP Paribas Fortis only a week ago."

Not only a fucking cow, Frank thought, but a fucking stupid cow with it.
"Another unfortunate coincidence, Mr McDonald?" Frank said nothing.
"Or a payment to your American co-conspirator?" There was nothing to
say, this was all just too ridiculous for words, certainly for any words that
Frank could think of now.

"And then there's the matter of your death threats made against the victim's friend, Monsieur Chaudier, with whom the victim was residing at
the time of his death. And who is also, I believe, your colleague."

"Ok, enough now" Frank stood up, "Fucking Renaud."

"Sit down, Mr McDonald, we're not finished. I've not spoken with Monsieur Chaudier yet, but I'm sure he'll be very interested to hear about your
frequently expressed desire to pick him up by the lapels and throw him
onto a train track."

"It was a joke," Frank said, realising too late that he should not have said
that, even though it was the truth.

"You do seem to have a particularly dark sense of humour, if I may say so"
The inspector took a sheet of paper from the file.

"And then" He paused again before delivering his coup de grace. "There's
your DNA test."

Frank looked down at the form that the Inspector held in his hand. Even
upside down, he recognised it. He had seen it, incomplete then, only yesterday afternoon.

Yesterday afternoon, before Philippe had died. Before Fiona killed him.

"Congratulations on becoming a father, Frank, if I may call you Frank."

He needed to be with Izi. He needed to wake up now and find himself
beside her.

The Inspector continued, he was enjoying himself. He was flying a kite,
but he was flying it well. And there was no sense in bringing it back down
to earth yet.

"Madame Anderson has been charged with several public order offences."
There was no harm in letting Mr McDonald sweat for another week or
two. Who did he think he was anyway? Another fool on the hill. And one
with a good deal more money than sense.

His statement would be interesting. It would make great TV. He might
even get to play the part of himself, but as a Chief Inspector, of course.

The Judicial Inquiry would find Monsieur Malibran's death to have been
an unfortunate accident. He had been in the wrong place at the wrong
time. He had deliberately put himself there. Same as the American woman, they both had it coming to them.

It would find that the policing of the demonstration had been appropriate, that the use of force had been proportionate, and that there had been no misconduct.

Hopefully, there would be no need for a Judicial Inquiry at all.

"Whether or not she will face more serious charges, and whether you will face any at all, of course, will depend on the statement that you will now dictate to me."

Frank was no longer angry. He was no longer even listening. He was Ana's father.

"The statement that you will now dictate to me, Frank." The Inspector repeated.

And he was desperate for a cigarette.

"But first, maybe you would like to step into the courtyard for a moment for some air."

# 27. Scotland v Croatia

Ana was spending the evening with her school friend, Marie. Marie's mother was Croatian, her father was Belgian, and they, and Marie's big brother, Tomaz, were all supporting Croatia tonight.

Ana and Marie had no great interest in football. And though they were happy enough to identify as Croatian or half Croatian, and though they enjoyed holidays with their grandparents, and their aunts and their uncles and their cousins, neither felt it was any big deal.

Everyone at school was half something, though Marie and Tomaz were two of only a few who were half Belgian. So everyone had at least two teams to follow in Euro 2020, which at last, one year later, was now finally a reality.

So far Ana seemed to be taking the turning of her world on its head, if not quite in her stride, then a step at a time, or at least she gave the impression that she was managing to do so.

Her father's funeral had been a small gathering of family and friends. Izi's parents did not make the trip from Zagreb, and Izi and Frank had agreed that he should not attend.

The Inspector put in a brief appearance at the graveside. As did Fiona, who at least had the good grace not to stay longer and to keep herself to herself. Izi did not talk to her, and told Ana, when she asked, only that she was a friend of her father's.

Whilst not a part of the education system, or the healthcare system, which, for all that Belgians complain about them, are a good deal better than many places elsewhere in Europe, psychologues are in reality an important part of both.

That Ana had already been making regular visits to hers for a couple of years, even before the trauma of her parent's separation, was far from unusual.

Many of her school friends did the same, Marie included. Ana, and Izi also, were fortunate that they had a particularly good one.

Dr Lejeune, Caroline to Ana, had asked to see Frank just as soon as Izi had first spoken of him.

And despite Frank's reservations about any form of shrink, he had found her to be perceptive and helpful, perhaps even a little too much so.

She had seen Philippe of course also, both before and during the separation, and she had seen him with Ana, and Ana with her mother, and the three of them together.

Ana liked Caroline, and she trusted her. Caroline listened to her, of course, that was her job, but more often than not, she seemed to take Ana's side.

That was something that did not always meet with Izi's approval. If they had never exactly clashed, then that was only because Izi had backed off when she saw it coming.

More than once she had felt that Dr Lejeune was judging her, or disapproving of her, and that she was letting Ana know that, or at least allowing her to feel it.

Izi told Dr Lejeune about the paternity question, before she told Frank, in fact, and before she knew that he would agree to the test, which he was not compelled to do.

Dr Lejeune's advice was that although Ana would have to be told that Frank was her father, she had the legal right to be told in fact, she did not have to be told now.

She had coped well with the separation, though she was still inclined to take her father's part in that. But she was still grieving her father's death.

Or at least the death of the man that she had, for all of her life, believed to be her father. It wascertainly a very delicate situation for them all. And it was at least in Dr Lejeune's experience, entirely unprecedented.

She knew of no comparable situation, and nor did any of her colleagues. There seemed to have been no comparable case ever. There were certainly no case notes or published articles.

To complicate matters, there were also the circumstances, not only of her father's death at the hands of a woman who was Frank's ex-girlfriend, but the remaining possibility that she, and Frank with her, could yet face criminal charges.

So Ana would not be told now, but when? And by whom?

Frank was watching the game at De Valera's, an Irish Bar on Place Flagey. It was not somewhere that he went often unless to watch football, which was, after all, what it was for. Football, and rugby, and Frank was not a rugby fan.

It was not somewhere that Izi had ever been, but it was her idea that they come here together.

She was a fan of her national team, as all of her countrymen were. And she was an enthusiastic one, despite having had no great interest in football before the famous victory over England that had taken them to their first World Cup Final three years ago.

She wore a Croatia scarf, Frank was dressed in the vintage Archie Gemmel Argentina 78 shirt that had been a birthday gift from Peter Galbraith. But tonight he had chosen to wear it with jeans, and not a kilt, not even his drinking kilt, which he had left hiding at home in the wardrobe.

Partly because he had no wish to embarrass Izi anymore than was going to be strictly necessary, but partly because, despite the occasion, and despite the twenty-three years that had led up to it, he now found himself, understandably given recent events, not completely in the mood.

There were a couple of tables with other Croatians. They greeted Izi as one of their own and she greeted them similarly when she entered the bar. And then again when Croatia twice found the back of the net.

She knew how much tonight meant to Frank, and she knew how much he desperately needed, how much they both desperately needed, a night away from, well, away from everything.

It had been five weeks now.

De Valera's offered a dozen or more TV screens of varying sizes. The food, burgers and the like, was adequate, the service was good, and Frank knew the manager.

Or at least the manager knew him. He had watched the Czech Republic game here, and the 0-0 draw with England and he was quietly confident that Scotland might yet get the win they needed to progress from the group stage for the first time in their history.

That is to say that he had not yet entirely given up hope, about the football at least. But, try as he might, and as he did, he still could not put, well, everything, out of his mind.

Izi was over Philippe's death, not that, if she were honest, there had ever been that much to get over, not at least about the actual death itself. If anything that had come as, well if not a relief, exactly, then something not far from it.

She worried about Ana, but she knew that her daughter was already a tough young woman, born of the same blood as she was, and as her mother and her father before her.

She was almost the same age now as Izi had been that weekend when she had sat in her father's study. Struggling to comprehend his words and what they meant, as the world that she had known began to crumble around her. She would be ok. She would not pass her teenage years in a city at war, or her youth in exile. She would know, as she herself had known, and knew still, the love of parents who loved each other every bit as much as they loved her.

If anything she was more worried about Frank. Although he affected to have put the interview with the Inspector out of his mind, it was obvious that he had not.

It was clear that he could not go back, but he could not seem to go forward either.

He wanted Ana to know that he was her father, he wanted everyone to know that he was Ana's father. He wanted everyone to know that he had had no part at all in Philippe's death.

He wanted everyone to know that he was not responsible for Fiona, or for what she had done.

But in truth, he did not yet entirely believe that that was the case. The Inspector, and his kite flying, had at least succeeded in doing that job well. The fact that it was him, and not Izi, that had now been placed on compassionate leave from work was not helping his mental health either. Although it was Eder who had signed it off, and who had, at least had the decency to call him, it had been Renaud's doing.

Izi meanwhile, had spoken with her mother about the case, as much as a petitioner to a judge as a daughter to a mother, though she had not told Frank that she had done so. She had sent her a copy of his statement, and she had told her what she knew about the circumstances of the interview, and about the behaviour of the Inspector.

Her mother agreed that it all sounded a bit odd. She said that she would talk to some people. She was fond of Frank and she was happy that he and Izidora had finally found their way back to each other.

And she certainly had no wish to see the father of her grandchild branded as a killer, far less convicted as a murderer.

Croatia 2-1 Scotland, Scotland were going home. Home before the postcards, as the joke had it, once again.

And there he was again. Steve Clarke's unmistakably Ayrshire face, looking down on Frank and Izi, from every screen in the room, as he acknowledged the stoic applause of The Tartan Army at Hamden Park on that chilly, wet June evening. Scotland had not been bad. They had drawn against England only three days before, after all. But Croatia had been better, and The Czech Republic too.

One of the Irishmen at the next table, who had been lending vocal support to what history at least knew to be the doomed cause that was a Scotland win, put his hand on Frank's shoulder: "Do you follow Scotland at the rugby as well?"

To which Frank, with what little good humour remained, could only reply "Do I not look like I've suffered enough?"

As the father of a Croatian, though, he was, he supposed, now allowed at least mixed feelings about the result. And it had not, in all honesty, been a surprise.

He paid the bill and they left De Valera's as the last remnants of the Tartan Army continued to sing Yes Sir I Can Boogie in the rain.

Izi pulled Frank towards her to shelter him under her umbrella. "They lost," she said. "What do they do when they win?" Frank thought for a moment, exaggerating the fact that he was doing so, for comic effect. And then he said, "You know, I have absolutely no idea, there isn't all that much in the way of precedent".

She laughed and she kissed him. "And what's with the 'they?' I'm still Scottish, you know, and our daughter is half Scottish too now, don't forget."

And she kissed him again, and they stopped walking, and she stopped laughing. And her eyes looked into his and she said: "you do want this, don't you, Frank, all of it?".

They walked on, past the shuttered and deserted funfair across the road on Place Flagey, and despite the unquestioned, unquestionable, utter certainty of his answer, Frank felt a melancholy, a familiar, age-old, Scottish melancholy return to him.

It carried him back in its mist in his mind. Back to his father, now Ana's grandfather, even in death, back to his father's funeral, back to Troon, back to the beach.

Back inevitably, inescapably, to Fiona. Though, of course, he knew now that not all memories are always true. You can forgive, but you cannot forget. Or is it the other way around? Why is it that feelings return without warning to haunt you like songs? If only there was a rhyme for forgiveness he thought.

They turned the corner into Chaussee de Vleurgat and they climbed the steep hill to Avenue Louise.

In silence in the rain.

At the top of the hill, Frank a little breathless now, they crossed the street. Izi almost losing her footing for a moment on the wet tram rails, before Frank took her arm. She put on her mask, and she joined the queue at the counter of the Friterie Vandermeulen.

They had shared fish and chips as the match kicked off, but they had both had several beers since then, and it had been an emotionally charged evening for both of them, not least of it the football.

Frank stepped away into the car park. He lit a cigarette and he turned on his phone. There were a couple of dozen or so mails which he ignored and a thread of SMSes from Peter Galbraith about their fate as members of The Tartan Army.

And there was one voice message.

The Inspector was sorry to call him so late in the evening. He apologised for the delay in getting back to him, but he had only just received the news himself.

After some consideration, The Ministry of Justice had now decided that there would not be a Judicial Inquiry after all. There was no need.

The circumstances of Monsieur Malibran's accidental death were clear, and not disputed by his next of kin. Nor by Madame Anderson, whose statement had entirely concurred with Franks.

The charges against her would, in the circumstances, now be left to rest on the file.

There would be an internal police inquiry, but it would have limited terms of reference and no power to order further investigations, nor to bring charges.

The Inspector thanked Frank for his cooperation, and he apologised for any distress that might have been caused to him.

He assured him that the matter was now closed and that he would not be hearing from him again.

He sounded a little drunk, Frank thought.

# 28. Croatia v Belgium

The Croatian Justice Minister was an old friend of Izi's mother. The two women had attended law school together, and both had graduated with honours. They had both worked together as lawyers in the former Yugoslavia.

They had lived through the war together as comrades, and as neighbours in Zagreb. And they had lost more than one friend in common.

They were almost the same age. And they were both now close enough to retirement to no longer have to exercise quite the same degree of caution in what they said and what they did as they once had. Both were formidable women, and both enjoyed a reputation for not suffering fools gladly, if at all.

The Minister knew her opposite number in Brussels well. Both had been in post for some years and he had often hosted her and her fellow Ministers at meetings and their attendant receptions and dinners.

She knew him well enough certainly to pick up the phone and call him. And for him to call her back immediately that morning, despite all that he had on his desk. Being a Minister in a small EU country had advantages.

Being a Justice Minister during a lockdown had not been an easy job or a pleasant experience for either of them, they agreed. But protests, and the tricky subject of the policing of protests, was not a subject that was going to go away now that the lockdowns were mostly over.

As the world seemed to be tentatively returning to some sort of normality, the pandemic had left behind a new, or at least a much greater, suspicion of government and authority in its wake.

He was under pressure, even from some within his Government, for a Judicial Enquiry into the death of a protestor at the second La Boum. Phone camera footage was circulating on social media and none of it showed the actions of the police that afternoon in a good light. In some parts of the press, Monsieur Malibran was gaining a reputation as something of a martyr.

And so The Belgian Minister of Justice was a little surprised to find that the purpose of the call from his opposite number in Zagreb was to raise her concerns about the treatment of the family of a Croatian citizen during enquiries into the circumstances of Monsieur Malibran's death. But he was certainly interested in what she had to say. He promised that he would look into it. And no sooner than he ended the call, that is what he did.

It had been clear from the outset that there were only two ways to deal with the La Boume problem.

But he was grateful to now have been alerted to the fact that someone, somewhere, and somewhere close to home, seemed to have been flying some sort of a kite in favour of a third.

A Judicial Enquiry could be held into the policing of La Boum with the possible, indeed in his estimation, the likely, finding that the use of disproportionate force by the police had been a contributory factor in the death of Monsieur Malibran.

Or else some internal Police Inquiry might be held instead. Monsieur Malibran's death would be found to have been accidental, and he and his name would quickly be forgotten.

The possibility that he had been murdered, or that he had been the victim of a conspiracy to murder that included the family of a Croatian diplomat known to the Croatian Minister of Justice was, well, this was the stuff of a TV Crime Drama.

He would let The Commissioner of Police find whoever it was whose fevered imagination that had come from, and they would face the consequences.

But at least the rest of it was now relatively straightforward. A Judicial Enquiry, and the likely finding that the police had used disproportionate force? Or no Judicial Enquiry, and a tragic accident?

The decision was a Ministerial one, and technically, at least his, to make. But he would not make it. No, he would take it to Cabinet. And in the unlikely event that it was to go to a vote, then he would abstain. It would not be his decision, and so, whatever the outcome, he would survive, as he had always done.

The Inspector, it turned out, had already been on The Commissioner of Police's radar for some time. As well as being suspected of passing confidential details of enquiries to the press, he was, it now emerged, registered with a Brussels talent agency as a film extra, as well as working with a film production company on story development for TV Crime Drama.

He was also the cousin of a close friend of Monsieur Malibran, a Brussels functionary and a colleague of the Scotsman suspected of being the instigator of the Croatian conspiracy.

Even the Minister had to read the Commissioner's note a couple of times before he could make much sense of it all. The Inspector, as luck would have it, was also soon due to face a promotion board.

119

Perhaps, the Commissioner suggested, it was now an appropriate time for the promotion board to recognise the Inspector's creative talents, and his natural flair for publicity, by making him up to the rank of Chief Inspector.

And then recommending his immediate transfer to an administrative role in the Road Traffic Division, in Liege, or Charleroi, perhaps.

The Minister did not relay any of these details to Zagreb. He had no wish to make himself, or his government, or his country, look ridiculous.

But he did thank her for the valuable information that she had been able to provide. He reassured her that he had now looked into the matter thoroughly and that, yes, it did appear that some irregularities had occurred.

He asked her to give his apologies to Madame Ludovic and her family, to let her know that appropriate action had been taken and that the matter was now closed.

Frank had no personal prior experience of the power of a family matriarch, nor, of course, of the fierce loyalty of a mother finding her child in any way close to danger.

He would never know the detail of what had happened to him and why.

But he would be eternally grateful to Mrs Ludovic, and he would be forever in her debt. Which, of course, is just exactly the way that matriarchs the world over like it to be.

Perhaps there was no answer, perhaps there was no question either, perhaps it had all just been a series of, as the Inspector himself had put it, unfortunate coincidences.

Whatever it had been, it was all over now. And all without Frank ever knowing how close he had been to the truth about Renaud's part in it all.

Frank's predicament having now been resolved, Izi's mother turned her energies to the question of her granddaughter's wellbeing, a word she used only, of course, in its strictly literal sense.

She would invite Ana to spend the summer with her and her grandfather on the coast. Without her mother and father.

## 29. In Dreams

Michael Palin was on a train, it was an old train. Perhaps it was The Orient Express. It was in Croatia, or it could have been Scotland, or it might have been India.

Ana was with him, and her friend Marie. They were sitting at a table that had been dressed with a starched linen table cloth, as if for lunch.

They were playing a card game.

Bill sat opposite them, with a drawing board balanced between his knee and the edge of the table, his pen, pencil, eraser and ink arranged in front of him, as he drew and redrew the scene.

He was dressed as a priest and wearing spiked golf shoes. Frank appeared along the corridor, wearing the suit that he had worn to Bill's funeral. But it had silver buttons on it now, and a crest sewn into the breast pocket.

He carried a white cloth folded over his arm.

He was wheeling a trolley, from which he served ham and tomato sandwiches, scotch eggs, pork pies, and tea, and lemonade from a glass jug.

Bill paid him, hundreds of pounds, in large notes, which he took from a holdall on the rack above.

Beyond the carriage window there were mountains and castles, and then a forest, and then a city, and for a moment Frank thought that he recognised the spires of its University buildings.

But it was gone. They passed through a long tunnel and into a cloud. A cloud of steam, for the train now, certainly, was a steam train.

It emerged at the seaside where children were building sandcastles. It stopped at a station, a small station, that stood on a small hill, in a small seaside town.

Hercule Poirot was waiting for them on the platform. He was with Izi's father. Behind them a dark-haired woman sat on a bench, rolling a cigarette. Hercule Poirot was the Hercule Poirot of Frank's youth, the actor David Suchet. Michael Palin knew him, and Bill did also. They waved to each other, as the two men boarded the train, each carrying leather monogrammed suitcases.

Ana did not recognise her grandfather. He was dressed as a Belgian Policeman. There had been a murder. A brutal murder.

A man, whom nobody seemed to know, had been fatally struck by a blow to the back of the head, with a library book.

Poirot was questioning Frank and his colleague Fabrizio. Izi's father was taking notes. But they were not notes, they were poems. He was drinking cognac.

They were in Chez Martine. The Kilmarnock Football Team sat on the benches opposite. There was a trophy on the table. They were singing 'I just want to be your teddy bear.'

Steve Clarke was serving behind the bar. Peter Galbraith was washing glasses.

They kissed. Peter Galbraith was Renaud. He was on the roof of a hospital smoking a cigarette. A jet of water curved above him and formed a rainbow. An ambulance passed by below on a railway track. But it was a train, and then an aeroplane.

Frank woke suddenly. He was sitting bolt upright strapped to a chair.

The Slovakian steward took his two empty miniatures of Famous Grouse and his empty bottle of Highland Spring Water from the seat back table in front of him, and he put them in the trash bag.

He did not recognise Frank, but Frank recognised him.

Frank got up and went to the toilet. He took a pee and he washed his hands and face. The dream was fading away but fragments of it still played in his mind's eye. And, like watching trailers for a film that you've already seen, he found that comforting.

All that he had been through now seemed to make perfect sense to him.

He returned to his extra legroom seat and he strapped himself in. Ryanair Flight FR 7353 would be landing in Edinburgh in ten minutes.

# 30. Back To The Drawing Board

This interview would be much easier. Frank was better prepared, and however, it turned out this morning he would not find himself accused of having killed someone.

The final decision would be Eder's, but all involved in the selection, including Frank, the candidate, the only candidate so far as he knew, had agreed that it would not be necessary for Eder to make the journey to Edinburgh to interview someone that he already knew well.

The post was that of a Deputy Director, a significant promotion for Frank. The decision to keep the Parliament's Liaison Office in Edinburgh open following Brexit, and to expand and strengthen it, had been controversial. But it had also been a rare display of foresight.

Support for Scottish Independence was gathering pace again. And at the same time what hostility there had been to the idea in Brussels was receding.

Frank, Eder had told him, on his return from compassionate leave, and in the strictest confidence, could perhaps come to play a valuable role in the accession of our next member state, if that was how things were to turn out in the end.

For now, it would remove the unresolved question of the status of Frank's residency in Belgium, although there was now another way of doing that, which Izi had already, if not yet properly discussed, then at least put on the table for future discussion.

It would have the advantage of removing Frank from any further direct contact with Renaud which was, they agreed, now probably best for all concerned. And, of course, Eder had assured him, he would be required to make regular visits to Brussels, where the door would always be open for him, perhaps, to one day return.

For once, it seemed to Frank, as he tucked into his full Scottish breakfast in the restaurant of The Angel's Share Hotel that morning, there did not seem to be any obvious downside to any of it.

The future looked bright, brighter than the weather anyway, which was whipping an icy wind in off the North Sea, as it could do in Edinburgh, even in August.

Frank was a West Coast Man and had never lived in Edinburgh. And though the capital was only forty minutes on the train from Glasgow, its climate was colder and drier.

Scotland, he had told Izi, who had never been there, combines the temperature of Poland with the rainfall of Indonesia, but at least you do get to choose between them.

The people were quite different too. Like the weather, they were also colder and drier in Edinburgh.

As the joke had it, if you found yourself in someone's home in Glasgow in the early evening, the hosts would invite you to eat with them with the words: "You'll have your tea?"

But were you to find yourself in the same situation in Edinburgh, they would not, saying instead: "You'll have had your tea."

It was a bit like the Belgians and the Dutch and the tomato soup.

But he was getting ahead of himself. Where he would live, and whether or not Izi and Ana would live there with him were questions for another day. All the same, they were questions that excited him, and whatever the answers would turn out to be, the future looked bright.

The interview turned out to be a formality, and also pleasantly informal. There was no interview panel, as there would have been in Brussels. There was no one from Brussels present at all.

Frank had expected someone from HR at least to have made the trip, and no one from the London office either.

A young man showed Frank into the Director's office, where the Director, Jim Cochrane, sat alone at his desk. He was a man that Frank had met on a couple of occasions, but he did not know him.

He had not been involved in the drafting of the narrative or the execution of the election campaign.

The British had come late to that. Had Brexit gone to plan then the UK would have left before the vote anyway.

Cochrane invited Frank to take a seat on the sofa opposite his desk and then came over to join him. He had no papers with him, there was no sign of Frank's file or even his CV. This was either a very good sign, or else a very bad sign. Frank could not yet read which.

A tray of coffee was already set on the table between them. Frank poured himself a cup and then offered one to Cochrane.

Cochrane began by telling him that he was due to retire in two years. This was news to Frank, it was not something that Eder had mentioned.

He did not sound particularly interested in who would succeed him, but it would have to be a Scot, of course. Perhaps it would be Frank, he suggested.

In the meantime, the rest of his tenure would be a gradual, but thorough, preparation for whoever that would be.

It was considered likely now, in Brussels, and not only by Eder, that the next Director would be in post when the question of Scotland's accession as a member state arose.

Scotland, was a strongly pro-EU country, more so than he had thought, he said, He had been as surprised by the strength of the Remain vote in Scotland, as by the size of the leave majority south of the border.

"The Nationalists like to talk to Brussels directly," he said. "And rightly so, they are the Government, after all, and it's not our job to get in their way."

"The others don't seem to want to talk to anyone at all. Not that there's any of them left these days that are much worth talking to anyway" he said.

"Stay away from politics in any shape or form, even your local council, actually especially your local council, ignore the London office, they're not part of the big picture going forward. And the London press for that matter too."

Frank had expected that there might be a bit more to it.

"There's not much any of us can do about the present mess, I'm afraid. And don't get me started on tourism, the hotels, and the bars and the restaurants, there's just no staff now. Brexit wasn't the reason everyone went home, no, that was mostly down to COVID, but it's the reason they're not coming back, that's for sure."

There was a sadness in his voice. A realisation of just what a mess it all was. He stopped for a moment. There was a mournful silence. And then, almost as an afterthought, he mentioned that there was also some work with schools and colleges, but that there were people who would look after all that for him.

"Keep Eder happy, he trusts you, and I respect his opinion. Spend as much time in Brussels as you want, the more the better, you have a family there, I believe."

I have a family in Brussels, Frank ran the thought through his mind. And he smiled.

"And sit tight and wait for another Independence vote."

Cochrane smiled and rose to his feet. "It'll come, eventually." He fist-bumped him. And then shook him firmly by the hand. "Welcome aboard, Frank."

The young man who had shown him in reappeared, summoned, no doubt, by the same sort of hidden button arrangement that Eder employed. Perhaps Frank would get one of them too, he thought, now he was to be a Deputy Director.

"This is Alan Kerr, our admin assistant, Alan, Frank McDonald. Frank will be joining as from Brussels, as our new Deputy Director."

Frank stepped out into Holyrood Road. Feeling more than a little pleased with himself.

The wind had dropped and the sun was out. He walked up the Cowgate and turned left at the Belhaven Brewery, which gave him an idea, it was almost midday and a respectable time, in Edinburgh certainly, for a man's first pint of the day.

He knew just exactly where he wanted to go now, and what he wanted to do.

He carried on down past the tourist crowds browsing the Kilt Shops and examining the itineraries and the prices of the Castles of Outlander Tours. They were noticeably thinner this first post-pandemic summer. But it was good to see some of them back anyway.

Over The North Bridge, past Waverley Station, and then up West Register Street.

And in the public bar of The Cafe Royal, he ordered a pint of Independence.

## 31. A Red Red Rose

Frank took a book from the shelf in the front room.

Bill had never been much of a reader and the choice available to him was not extensive. But pretty much every home in Scotland has at least one volume of the works of Robert Burns.

And pretty much every one of them contains My Love Is Like A Red Red Rose.

He set it down on the table, where he had already placed a bottle of ink and a couple of Bill's pens. And some pieces of graph paper which he had carefully cut from the one unused yellowing roll that remained among those of his father's drawings that he had left.

He had still not decided what was to be done with Harling Drive. Troon to Edinburgh was not a viable daily commute, but perhaps his new role would not require that of him.

It was not ideally placed for regular trips to Brussels either, there being no direct flight from Glasgow, but perhaps he could spend weekends here.

Perhaps he would get himself a season ticket for Kilmarnock. Perhaps he would take up golf. It would not be unusual for a man at his time of life. His father had once told him that it was a game that was best played against yourself. A mind game, so perhaps, he thought, it might suit him. Perhaps it might even turn out to be in his blood.

Or maybe life as a family man might not leave him time for such things.

He opened the book and he set about the task of transcribing the poem. Frank was just old enough to still have been taught handwriting at Irvine Primary, but he did not have his father's touch.

It took him a while to get the feel of the pen, but he was in no hurry. Izi would not be here till this evening.

'O my love is like a red, red rose that's newly sprung in June. O my love is like the melody.

That's sweetly played in tune'.

His first attempt looked broken and scratchy and his second was over-inked, as though a spider had fallen into the ink bottle and then escaped and run across the page.

He tried the other pen, which felt heavier in his hand, and this time he took more care with the ink, taking not too much, and not too little.

'So fair art thou, my bonnie lass, so deep in love am I. And I will love thee still, my dear. Till a' the seas gang dry'.

It looked better this time, neater and more even, but the edge of his hand had smudged the ink.

He tried again.

'Till a' the seas gang dry, my dear. And the rocks melt wi' the sun. I will love thee still, my dear.

While the sands o' life shall run'.

And again, and again, and again, until he had covered both sides of all but one of the sheets of graph paper. By now it looked almost professional, he thought, or at least more than acceptable.

But did the verses read better in two lines or four? They were set in four in the book, he would go with that.

It was late afternoon by the time he had finished, but he was pleased with the result.

He thought for a moment about how best he should sign it, before deciding that anything more than Frank and an x would be redundant. Burns had said the rest, he thought, more eloquently than he could ever have managed himself.

He went out into the garden. And he cut a single red rose from the bush in the rockery by the garage, 'and the rocks melt wi the sun' indeed.

The bush that he had never once noticed was there until the night before. He went back into the front room. He placed the rose on the table, and, the ink now dry, he carefully folded the paper and put it in an envelope.

He wrote: 'For Izi' on it and he placed it beside the rose on the table in the front room, the room reserved for the importance of certain days and certain rituals.

He put Burns back on the shelf, and he tidied away the pens and the ink.

She called him when she landed in Edinburgh, and then again from Glasgow. She was loving Scotland, she told him, so far so good.

Everyone was so smiley, but she was, as Frank had predicted, finding it difficult to understand exactly what people were saying. She was getting on the train at Glasgow Central now, and she would be in Troon in forty minutes.

The sun shone, but there was already an autumn chill in the evening air. Izi wore her green quilted coat and white woollen scarf. More simply beautiful, and more irresistibly attractive, yes, and sexier and more completely desirable than anyone that Frank McDonald had ever before had the good fortune to share a moment of his life with.

Across the street, the Saltire and The Union Jack hung limply from the

Walker hall. He pointed them out to her, though she knew well enough what both were and what both meant. Though she had always shared his distrust of flags and anthems, they both agreed that his job, his mission, was to one day, and one day soon, see the European flag hang there. In place of the Union Jack.

And they drank to that. And then they drank to Izi's mother, and to Ana, who was doing just fine, Izi said.

She had taken the news about her old father, and about her new father, well. Better than either Izi or her mother, had expected.

She was not a child, perhaps she had already known the truth. Anyway, she was looking forward to getting to know Frank. Perhaps, Izi said, they should invite her and her grandmother here.

There was, Frank agreed, no perhaps about it, and no question about it either. They could come whenever they wanted, as soon as they wished, next week maybe if they were free.

And they drank to that too. And they ordered a second bottle of the Chablis, which wasn't bad, even though it was a good deal more expensive than the last one that they had drunk together in Chez Franz. And they ate their fish and chips, which were certainly a good deal better than the last ones they had eaten together in De Valera's.

It had been a long day and Izi was tired. They walked from the Tides Cafe back up Academy Street and into Harling Drive, while the jukebox in Frank's head paraphrased The Green Green Grass Of Home, substituting Izi's name for that of Mary.

The jukebox, at least, was no musical snob and at least it had the good grace to fade out before it got to the bit about waking up in prison.

The walk seemed to have taken the edge of Izi's tiredness and she was happy to accept his offer of a nightcap, a whisky, of course, in the front room. And she was happy to accept his gifts, very, very happy. She knew herself well enough to know that she had never been much of a romantic and to know why.

But she had always been pleased that Frank was, and it gladdened her heart now to see the evidence here before her eyes that, despite all that he had been through, the true romantic in him still flourished.

She was happy also that the beautiful, heartfelt, declaration of his love was not the prelude to the proposal of marriage that she had feared, and that Frank himself had only this morning considered, only to think better of it. The gesture, for what more is marriage now than that, that both of them knew would only be made because of the responsibility of parenthood, or else as the means by which Frank could regain his European citizenship.

Not that that was something that should, or would, not at least remain on the table.

She loved him, though he was not an easy man to love, and she hoped that they would spend the rest of their lives together, but should she marry him, could she marry him?

It was a question that she had asked before. A question that in some ways Ana had answered.

The next day they woke early, and they made love. And then they made breakfast. And then they took a few of Bill's clubs and a bag of balls across the road and Frank asked the green keeper if, as beginners, they might play a few practice holes on the Lothian.

If a little grudgingly, and if they let games play through, of course, and if they were done in an hour or so, then yes, he said, he thought that would probably be ok.

"You can play the back nine, there's only a couple of games out," he said. "It's Frank is it no? Frank McDonald? "I kent yer faither."

Once out of earshot, Izi told Frank that the man reminded her of a character from Harry Potter, and she asked him why he spoke in what, to her, sounded like Dutch.

And Frank explained that from what little he knew, he thought that Trainspotting was probably a more appropriate point of reference. And that the Scots and the Dutch did share some similarities, but that fortunately these were mostly confined to language.

Scots use the Dutch verbs to ken and to kiek for to know and to take a look, and both speak of a short local shopping trip, to buy milk or bread, for example, as doing the messages.

She did not though enquire at all about the game that they were about to play. Nor did she mention that, since she had been on her own without Ana, she had been spending her time studying golfing tutorials on Youtube.

Her drive at the short tenth was the first time that she had ever hit a golf ball.

And it was a lot more impressive than Frank's, which he shot almost vertically into the air before it landed barely twenty yards in front of him "Try and keep your head down." She said. Her second shot rolled onto the green and she putted out for her par.

Frank knew well enough when he'd been dealt the role of the sucker.

He was struggling to see the mind game in this, though he did seem to be mostly playing it against himself. If it was in his blood then it was as weak as the family tree was short. They did not, in the end, play all nine holes, their progress was slow, and the course was already getting busier. Izi seemed perfectly at home, but Frank knew that he was embarrassing himself, and her.

On those that they played, he played a stroke or two, either off the tee, or else a couple of puts, or sometimes both, but not the difficult stuff in-between where he either simply picked up his ball, or else abandoned it to the wastelands where it landed.

Until they stood on the eighteenth tee, and Izi finally persuaded him to give it one more try, for her. "Just keep your head down." She said.

And so he did, and the club made a beautiful pinging sound, like someone ringing a bell, and the ball flew low and straight, and it landed in the middle of the fairway, where it bounced once, then twice, and then it rolled on for another twenty yards or so.

His second shot wasn't too bad either, it was certainly much easier playing off the short, freshly mown grass on the fairway than in the heather and gorse beyond it.

But his third shot, which was, theoretically at least, just a short chip to the green, needed four attempts before it eventually got there. Where Izi, there in two, was now waiting for him, and where to his surprise, and hers, Frank deftly stroked a twenty-foot put straight into the hole.

"Beginner's luck," she said. And she laughed. Frank replaced the flag. And they shook hands, as even he knew that golfing etiquette demanded.

"A good thing Bill never had to play you for money." He said. And she laughed again. And they kissed. And he knew that he loved her, and she knew that she loved him.

And, warmed by that knowledge, they went and they sat on the wooden bench by the eighteenth green, and they shared a cigarette. And they looked across the road at the house on Harling Drive."Do you think that you can ever see us living here?" Frank said.

And she thought for a moment, and she said, "I think that I can see us living in lots of places. I can see us living here, and I can see us living in Brussels, and I can see us living in Croatia, on the coast."

And Frank knew then, at that moment, that you can only ever go back to go forward, and that you can never go back to finish things, but only to begin them again.

"And I can see us living in places that we've never even been." And he knew then that this was not an end, but a beginning. A beginning of something that had never really ended, for either of them, if that made any sense.

And he knew also then, that although her faith was constant, his was not. And that what she believed absolutely, he still sometimes doubted, despite himself. But whether or not that mattered, and whether or not that would ever matter, that, he did not know.

And what was to become of them, that, he could not tell.

As for Fiona, he did not doubt that she would have found another lover. But he surprised himself to hope that she was happy. As happy as he was today.

She had been right about a couple of things though, a couple of very important things.

Fear is the disease, and truth is the cure.

With thanks to Sabine Allaeys, Cigdem Y Mirol, Fabrizio Nicolucci (Design), Kardama Pedalbxl (Photography) and Guy Van Laere.

First published in November 2022
by mychoiceofwords.online

This edition
by **Paragon** - March 2023
ISBN: 978-1-78222-987-2

Ingram Content Group UK Ltd.
Milton Keynes UK
UKHW021217190323
418799UK00008B/27

9 781782 229872